The Vault was the first time Logan had opened it, even without flipping on the light switch, thanks to the gaping hole Seti had made in the door. Bright light from the main room streamed in, glinting off the golden sarcophagus.

The lid had been tossed to the side, landing end up against one of the walls. A spider web of long, jagged cracks laced through the golden effigy, heaviest at the head where they obscured the sculpted face.

One look told Logan that the sarcophagus was empty. Nevertheless, Logan ducked into the room, first peering carefully into the empty tomb then into all the shadowed corners. He crawled behind the sarcophagus, checking every inch of the floor, looking for the mummy. He banged on the walls, listening for any hollow echo that might indicate a hidden doorway or passage.

But there was no trace of the mummy anywhere, and no way that Logan could find for it to have been spirited out. For that matter, there was no way he could find for Seti to have gotten into the locked room except through the door he had shattered. It was as if the mummy had vanished into thin air. That unbelievable but undeniable observation posed a problem for Logan's pragmatic mind.

Logan was a scientist, a researcher. Methodical, unlikely to jump to conclusions, he had been trained to carefully study the evidence long and hard before posing an hypothesis. In this case, however, the facts spoke loud and clear – the mummy was gone.

This is a work of fiction. Names, characters, places, and incidents either are the product of the author's imagination or are used fictitiously. Any resemblance to actual events, locales, organizations, or persons, living or dead, is entirely coincidental and beyond the intent of either the author or the publisher.

TOP SHELF
An imprint of Torquere Press Publishers
PO Box 2545
Round Rock, TX 78680
© 2007 Kiernan Kelly
Cover illustration by Alessia Brio
Published with permission
ISBN: 978-1-60370-259-1, 1-60370-259-8

www.torquerepress.com

First Torquere Press Printing: January 2008
Second Printing: August 2008
Printed in the USA

**If you enjoyed Seti's Heart,
you might enjoy these Torquere Press titles:**

Diggers by Dallas Coleman

The Prince's Angel by Mychael Black and Shayne Carmichael

Riding Heartbreak Road by Kiernan Kelly

Soul Mates: Bound by Blood by Jourdan Lane

Tomb of the God King by Julia Talbot

Seti's Heart

Seti's Heart
by Kiernan Kelly

romance for the rest of us
www.torquerepress.com

Seti's Heart

PROLOGUE

5,000 years ago
Nile Valley, Egypt
Camp of the Children of Setekh

Blowing in fiercely across the dunes, the storm whipped the sand into a maelstrom of biting particles that could flay flesh from bone. Within moments, it could fill a man's lungs with sand, drowning him with the blood of the desert. In the animal skin tents of King Seti's tribe, his people cowered and quailed before the power of the sandstorm.

Seti alone stood against the onslaught, feet braced apart, chin held high. In the face of the storm's fury he was immoveable, as solid and unyielding as stone. Bare-chested, his only garment was a short linen loincloth. He stood with his head thrown back, his warrior braids whipping about his head: long, black, beaded scourges that flailed his face and sun-bronzed shoulders. Arms spread wide, he welcomed the wind, embracing its stinging wrath as one would embrace a son.

In a way, the tempest was Seti's child – he had nothing to fear from it. He had created it; it was he who had called the demon from its lair and unleashed it upon the land. The storm was Seti's shield, keeping him and his hidden from the eyes of his enemy. It was also his fist, his spear, and he wielded it without mercy, striking down all who dared defy him.

This time Seti's enemies had gone too far. Bidden by their god, they had stolen Seti's heart from him, had ripped it away and fed it, still beating and warm, to the jackals.

For that crime they would pay with their lives.

Ashai had been more than a lover, more than another pretty face in Seti's harem. He had been Seti's favorite, the only one capable of easing the tension from Seti's body and the worry from his mind with a single caress. Ashai's unusual, light-colored eyes, the color of an oasis, had twinkled with good humor even on the darkest of days. His smile and his arms had always been warm and inviting.

Seti had loved him above all others. For Ashai, Seti would have moved mountains, drained oceans. It was for Ashai that Seti had led his people across the dunes, seeking greener lands. Ashai had wished to settle, to build, to see their people grow fat and happy along the rich, fertile banks of the Nile; he grew weary of their nomadic life. In addition to wanting to grant Ashai his wish, Seti had found that the land along the great river to be rich in resources that would assure his camp's growth.

Each year it flooded, the waters nursing the earth. When the waters receded, the land was left ripe for planting. The wealth reaped from the river's bounty would assure Seti of a vast kingdom. He had led their people to this place, near where the wind rippled the waters of the great river.

But Seti's people were not the only ones to covet the fertile land. There were others, but they were of no more importance to Seti than the gnats that worried his beasts of burden. He had marched through their camps, leaving behind little but footprints in the sand. The dead were discarded; the living assimilated into Seti's camp. His numbers swelled.

Within Seti's own tribe there were those who were jealous of his riches, of his power. Seti's priests, grown envious and greedy, tired of Seti's rule. Wishing to make a weaker man king, one who they could manipulate, they sought out Seti's enemies and made a pact with them.

Together, they called upon Setekh, the god who had bestowed upon Seti's family their power; they lied and convinced Setekh that Seti had dishonored him by giving Ashai honors due only to the gods.

One night, when darkness had settled over Seti's camp like a thick, suffocating shawl, as Seti sat with his advisors readying for war, his enemies had stolen in and taken Ashai from him. Almost before Seti knew he was gone, Ashai's head was returned to Seti minus his beautiful green eyes, the name of the god Setekh carved into his forehead.

Seti's priests told him that the warning had been clear: Seti should seek to please no one but the gods; the land of the Nile was not to be his. Give over to his enemies, or be destroyed.

A King of his people, Seti was a warrior to be reckoned with, but more, he was a sorcerer. In his veins flowed an ancient magic, gifted to his bloodline in the time before time, before the gods had wiped the dust of the earth from their feet. A gift bestowed upon Seti's family by the very god for whom he was named, as was his father, and his father's father before him back through the mists of time.

That Setekh, the god to whom Seti owed his powers and who he and his ancestors had worshiped and burned offerings to was the same god who had demanded Ashai's blood as payment for Seti's disobedience, sent a rage unlike any Seti had ever known roaring through his blood.

The wind carried Seti's oath across the sand.

"SETEKH! YOU MISERABLE JACKAL! WHORE OF HORUS! MAY YOUR GENITALS SHRIVEL AND BE EATEN BY THE SWINE WHO WORSHIP YOU!" he bellowed, his voice barely audible above the fury of the storm. "I curse the day my ancestors first uttered your foul name! I denounce you! From this day forward I will seek out those who bow down before you and trample them beneath my sandals until at last there are none left! Until your existence is less than a memory, forgotten by the world! I swear this, upon my very soul!"

Screams rose from over the hill as the storm found Seti's enemies, the windborne sand flaying them, burying them alive. After a very long while the terrible din ceased, the howl of the wind the only sound remaining.

The wind grew fiercer, particles of sand whipping Seti's flesh like a cat o' nine, biting deep. Then suddenly, all stilled. Sand, airborne a heartbeat ago, fell in a cloudy curtain to the ground, the wind dying to less than a whisper. Before Seti, the warm air seemed to shimmer, becoming alive, taking solid form as a giant rose up before him.

Eyes as dark as the deepest pits of the underworld glared at Seti from within a face so gruesome that it could make the strongest man cower in fear. Reptilian, long jaws were filled with dagger-like teeth, eyes that glowed with an otherworldly power gleamed. Below his neck, a strong and perfect body towered against the buff desert dunes.

Setekh.

An arm slowly rose, pointing a long, graceful finger at Seti. "Arrogant dog! You dare threaten me and mine?" Setekh thundered, his voice reverberating deeply in Seti's bones, chilling him to his very core. "Death is too easy a penance for you. It is you who will be forgotten! Hungry, thirsty, lonely, you will live a half-life, doomed to suffer five thousand years of agony! Never will your ka rest in the afterlife! Such is the curse your insolence has brought down upon your head!"

From within the tents of Seti his people rose up, commanded by a god they had worshiped all of their lives. They surrounded Seti, bore him up and carried him into the tents, where soon the only sounds that pierced the silence of the night were his screams.

CHAPTER ONE

Present Day
New York City, NY
National Museum of Natural History
Culture Halls, Division of Anthropology

I'm sorry, Mr. Ashton. I'm afraid your qualifications didn't pass muster. Ms. Rush has secured the position as my assistant."

Logan's humble - if biased - opinion was that Dr. Noah Peterson didn't look sorry at all. In fact, the man looked as though he was barely suppressing a gloating grin. There had been a persistent rumor going around that Dr. Peterson had not wanted to take Logan on as an assistant for one simple reason, and it had nothing to do with Logan's qualifications. That reason, at least according to the water cooler gossips, was Peterson's disapproval of Logan's alternate lifestyle choices.

In other words, Peterson was homophobic with a capital "H", and Logan was as out as a fella could get short of having the word "gay" tattooed across his forehead.

Susan Rush, on the other hand, was blonde, curvaceous, and possessed qualifications that included an ass that was nearly legendary among the straight male staff of the museum.

Logan sighed. To be fair, Susan also had a degree, had been in the top ten percent in her graduating class, and had a ream of recommendations from her professors.

Peterson had been Logan's last hope at a prestigious department's assistant's position, albeit a tissue thin one. The only other spot left open in the Museum's Fellowship Program was as Lincoln Perry's assistant, a career move that would have Logan buried up to his nose hairs in the deepest, darkest dungeons of the Museum, from where neither Logan nor his career would ever again see the light of day.

But then again, even slaving away in the bowels of the Museum beat starvation and eviction, which were Logan's only other options.

Logan bit his tongue, swallowing the half-dozen clever and bitingly caustic accusations that popped into his head but which would only have served to assure his future flipping burgers in the Museum's cafeteria. Turning his back on the pompous, arrogant Curator of Anthropology, he walked away, his dignity in shreds but his employment – such as it was – still intact.

Stopping off in Administration, Logan expressed his interest in becoming Dr. Perry's assistant. Lord, he should have been an actor – not only had he managed to sound excited about becoming Second-In-Charge Of Dusty Crates and Moldy Junk, he'd also successfully ignored the Administration Clerk's look of incredulity. He could almost hear the question that must have teetered on the tip of her tongue - a live body volunteering to work for Perry? Logan had no doubts that the woman would run straight from work to the store to purchase the heaviest coat available, since all indications pointed to Hell freezing over.

When the door of Administration clicked closed behind him, it sounded like the thunderclap of doom to Logan. His fate sealed, there was only one thing left to do – drown his sorrows in pitchers of draft beer while listening to the sympathetic commiserations and ill-conceived advice of his friends.

"Jase? Hey, it's me," Logan said, his voice a little breathless as he left the Museum and hurried down the sidewalk heading toward a bar favored by lesser humans beings such as anthropology graduate students. "Let's put it this way – it went about as well as expected. I'm heading over to The Bones now."

The Bones was actually a small bar named Hogan's, rechristened by the museum scholars who frequented it. Located two blocks from the museum, the bar was housed behind a nondescript, red-bricked façade. Dimly lit and famous for its five-dollar pitchers of beer, it was a favorite among students and museum assistants who had deep thirsts but shallow bank accounts.

Logan settled himself into a booth near the back of the bar and ordered a pitcher. If he had his way, it would be the first of many.

"You shouldn't frown like that, Logan," Wendy said, setting a frosty pitcher of Budweiser and a mug on the table. "When your eyebrows knit together it makes you look like you have a unibrow. Plus, it'll give you wrinkles."

Wendy was well past sixty and had been a waitress at The Bones since it had first opened its door in 1968. She was practically an historical landmark, knew everybody and their business as well as she knew her own. Her hair, a steely gray that she refused to dye, was wrapped around the crown of her head in a thick, silver braid. Her eyes could be either kind or frighteningly hard, depending on the circumstances, but at the moment they were softened with compassion.

She'd taken a liking to Logan and his small group of friends, which meant a few free pitchers now and then and a great deal of smothering mothering the rest of the time.

"I'll try to keep that in mind, Wendy."

"What's wrong? C'mon, Logan. Spill," Wendy said, sliding her substantial rear into the booth next to Logan.

"Didn't get the fellowship slot in Anthropology," Logan confessed. He should have known that Wendy wouldn't give up until she had all the sorry details. In that way, she was worse than his mother. Then again, Logan's mother didn't usually serve her son pitchers of beer and tell him that he needed to get laid more often.

"Why the hell not? You've got a freakin' 4.0, made the Dean's List all four years running, and have a ton of internship hours under your belt. Who could beat that?" Wendy was nothing if not loyal, taking any setback Logan or his friends experienced as a personal affront.

"Somebody who has two things I don't have. Tits," Logan smirked, pouring himself a beer. He downed half of it, mopping up the foam that dripped down his chin with his sleeve.

"These are napkins," Wendy said sarcastically, pulling a handful out of the dispenser and handing them to Logan. "Useful new invention. Try some. Besides, tits are overrated. They're fine when you're twenty, but when gravity hits it's like having a couple of millstones hanging around your neck."

Logan chuckled despite himself. "Thanks."

"Seriously, that sounds like discrimination to me. Isn't there anything you can do? Somebody you can complain to? File a grievance or something?"

"Sure. I could file a formal complaint with the Museum Board. Demand an investigation, call for a hearing. Of course, that would be the one sure-fire way to lose any chance I might ever have at a full professorship. I'd be lucky if I could get a job selling postcards in the gift shop after that," Logan answered, polishing off his mug. He poured another, intent on becoming as drunk as possible in as little time as necessary. "Besides, she really does have better qualifications for the position."

"That sucks," Wendy said, shaking her head. "So what are you going to do now?"

"Take a fellowship with Dr. Perry. He's the Curator of-"

"Lincoln Perry?"

"You know him? I didn't think he ever came up from the Museum's basement long enough to make friends. For that matter, I didn't think he was capable of making friends. Antisocial-"

Wendy's hand shot out, smacking Logan upside the back of his head.

"Ow!"

"You keep a civil tongue in your head when you're talking about Lincoln Perry, Logan," she growled, waggling a finger at him. "He's a fucking dinosaur and he's got a really big bite. He's got more friends in high places than the Museum Director. If you're going to work for Perry, you'd better mind your Ps and Qs."

"How do you know Dr. Perry?" Logan asked, rubbing the back of his head. This was taking mothering a bit too far, but he was too curious to say anything to Wendy and risk insulting her.

"I've been here a long time, Logan. I know lots of people. But Lincoln Perry has been here even longer than I have. He's been working in that museum since Hector was a pup, knows everybody and everything in it."

"He's Curator of Relics, Wendy, which means he's a glorified stock boy who keeps track of junk accumulated by the Museum, but unworthy of display. Donations that meant a lot to benefactors, but little to the scientific world."

"Just you wait and see if I'm not right," Wendy huffed, sliding out from the booth just as Logan's friends showed up. "This can be a great opportunity for you, if you keep your nose clean and your lips glued to the old boy's ass."

"Okay, Wendy. Whatever you say," Logan sighed. He knew better, but there was no sense in arguing the fact anymore. All he wanted right then was to plunge face first into a barrel of suds.

Jason, Leo, and Chris stood by, patiently waiting for Wendy to extract herself from the booth. All three were self-described SSOLs - Serious Students Of Life, although Logan's definition was Seriously Shit Out of Luck. Whichever meaning of the acronym you subscribed to, it meant the same thing - that they were young academics with brand new sheepskins and empty bank accounts. Although Jason had landed an internship at Sloan-Kettering, he was living off his rapidly dwindling trust fund, and the other two didn't have a single job prospect between them. Still, they were supportive and had helped keep Logan's head above the black waters of despair on more than one occasion. Logan considered himself lucky to have their friendship and loved them all like brothers.

Each gave Wendy a brief, dutiful peck on the cheek, assuring them of at least one free pitcher that night, then slid into the booth.

"So, it's a no-go in Anthropology, huh?" Jason said as he scooted onto the bench seat next to Logan. Logan had known Jason the longest of the three, having been assigned to the same dorm room his first day in college. The two of them had been as thick as peanut butter for years. Sometimes Logan thought Jason knew him better than Logan knew himself. "Peterson is such an asshole."

"Please don't associate that man with one of my favorite parts of the human anatomy," Leo said, smiling as Wendy set a full pitcher and three more mugs on the table. His blue eyes twinkled mischievously; dimples deepening, making him look like an overgrown, platinum blonde pixie. "He gives assholes everywhere a bad name."

"What are you going to do now, Logan?" Chris asked. His brown eyes peered at Jason from behind the thick lenses of his horn-rimmed glasses. The most reserved of the trio, Chris had the looks of a supermodel and the personality of a wet sponge. Still, he was intelligent and kind, and had been Logan's friend since his first year of college.

"Well, I put in for the assistant slot with the Curator of Relics-"

"Perry? Are you kidding?" Leo protested. "That's a fucking death sentence, Logan. I can hear the bells tolling for your career now."

"Shut up, Leo. What else could he do?" Chris growled. Logan couldn't help but smile when Leo jumped as Chris' sharp elbow connected with his ribs. "Not everybody is content to live off of love, you know."

"You're going to meet a man."

"What?" Logan looked at Jason, whose eyes were wide and unfocussed, his expression gone blank. Jason seemed to stare through Logan, seeing something beyond him that no one else could see, and it was giving Logan a severe case of the creeps. He hated when Jason went Twilight Zone on them.

"Shit. Here we go – step right up and see Jason the Magnificent predict the future while juggling beer nuts and cocktail napkins," Leo said, rolling his eyes.

"A man with no heart."

"Oh, great. Let me guess – he's an out of work actor whose last gig was the Tin Man in a Rotary Club presentation of the Wiz, right? Just what I fucking need," Logan groaned, rolling his eyes. "C'mon, Jase. You know I hate it when you start with this psychic bullshit."

"You will give him what he needs most." Jason's voice was a flat monotone, without the slightest trace of inflection. Logan suppressed a shudder.

"It's more like psychic diarrhea. When he gets like this, he's got more shit coming out of his mouth than a sewer line," Chris said, waving his hand in front of Jason's face. "C'mon, man, snap out of it!"

"Earth to Jason, come in, Jason," Leo snorted. "A heartless man. Sounds like a fun date. Well, it could be worse, Logan. He could have said you were going to meet a woman and hop the fence."

"I'm not going to meet anybody, unless you mean Dr. Perry," Logan said. He drained the last of his beer, refilling his mug. White foam sloshed over the side of the mug, pooling on the table. "Right now, I couldn't afford to go on a date, and I certainly don't need anybody complicating my life. It's fucked up enough as it is." He gave Jason a shove. "Knock it off, Jason," he growled.

Jason blinked. "What happened?"

"You know damn well what happened. Why do you insist on playing these Psychic Hotline parlor games?" Chris asked, frowning. "It's getting old, Jason."

"Honest to God, I didn't even know I was doing it," Jason protested. He looked pale to Logan, and there were beads of sweat on his forehead, even though it was chilly in the bar. "One minute I was looking at Logan, and the next... Did I say something?"

"Yeah. You said I was going to meet a heartless man. What exactly did you see, Jase?" Logan prompted. There was something about Jason's expression that sent a shiver down Logan's spine, sobering him.

"I don't know. It was dark, and hot. Windy. There was

a lot of sand."

"Like on the beach?" Leo asked.

"No, more like the desert," Jason said. He lifted a mug to his mouth, his hand shaking so badly that beer slopped over the side onto his shirt.

"What else?" Logan prompted.

"There was a man. He was huge, like a fucking giant, and he had the head of an alligator," Jason said, sliding the back of his hand across his mouth. "I didn't understand what he was saying, but he was sorely pissed off about something."

"Sounds like Setekh, the Egyptian god of Chaos. That would probably make it a crocodile head, not an alligator, although no one's really sure what animal he was associated with. Why the hell would you channel him?" Chris asked. "He was the bad boy of the Egyptian pantheon."

"Hell, boys! Deserts, giants, and heartless crocodile men? Sounds like a party to me," Leo grinned.

Logan forced his lips to curl in a smile, but inside he was still feeling discomfitted. Jason's "prophecies" were usually vague, easily interpreted to fit neatly into anyone's life. Not this time. This time there had been something ominous in his voice, and it had chilled Logan right to the bone.

He lifted his mug, drinking deeply. The night was young and he was well into his second pitcher, but try as he might, Logan couldn't get his buzz back.

CHAPTER TWO

D r. Perry?" Logan called, edging his way past a gigantic wooden drum, chipped and pitted and layered with a half inch of dust. It looked to be of eastern origin, perhaps Japanese. The basement consisted of several dozen rows of ceiling-to-floor metal shelves, each one choked with boxes and crates. The mess spilled over into every corner of the large basement room, filling it completely and leaving very little room to walk.

Clearing his throat, Logan tried again, louder this time. "Dr. Perry?"

"Back here. Mind your step, boy, and don't touch anything!"

The voice was steady and firm, carrying none of the tremble usually associated with advanced age. However, the years had not been as kind to Lincoln Perry's body as they had to his voice. Stooped and slight, he was completely bald except for a monk's fringe of white hair that fell in thin wisps over the collar of the lab coat. One might be tempted to think he had more hair growing in his eyebrows than he did on the rest of his head. Bushy and blindingly white, his brows were wild and unkempt, shadowing eyes set deeply in a heavily wrinkled face.

But those eyes sparkled with intelligence as they turned

to meet Logan's. "You're my new ass?"

"I beg your pardon?"

"My new assistant. But until you've proven yourself to be brighter than the average lump of oatmeal, you're an ass." Perry cackled at his own wit, turning back to the task he'd been working on – labeling what Logan could see was a large, gray human bone of indeterminate age. "Make yourself useful and help me wrap this thing."

Logan moved, anxious to prove himself smarter than a bowl of Quaker Oats. He'd be damned if he'd spend the rest of the year labeled as Perry's ass. Carefully, he rolled out the thin gauze, helping Perry wrap the bone securely, placing it in a box. Perry sealed it, writing Homo sapiens, thighbone, circa 1920 on the cover with a black Sharpie.

"Why are we keeping a human leg bone from the twentieth century? It's not exactly an antiquity," Logan said, lifting the crate as Perry instructed, carrying it between the rows. "There are graveyards full of bones like these everywhere."

"Why don't they ever send me someone with half a brain?" Perry sniffed, shooting Logan a haughty look as he led him between the rows. "It's not an antiquity now, but what about three thousand years from now? There were graveyards full of bones in ancient Egypt, Greece, and Rome, too, you know. Ever heard of the catacombs? But you wouldn't question my storing one of those bones."

Okay, so Perry was a nutcase, Logan decided. He must have spent too many years down in the dungeons breathing in the dust and mold. Logan sighed. If the last five minutes were any indication, it was going to be a long, long year.

"Put it up there, third shelf down from the top," Perry ordered, pointing to a spot on a shelf well above Logan's head.

Logan tucked the box under one arm and manhandled a ladder over to where Perry stood, waiting impatiently, tapping his foot. Climbing up, he wedged the box between another labeled Branding iron, Wyoming, circa 1800, and one that read Jawbone, Canis lupis familiaris, circa 1994.

There didn't seem to be any rhyme or reason in the storing of items. No alphabetical order, no grouping according to Genus, nada. Just stuff, most of it worthless, randomly stuck into whatever space could be found to accommodate it.

"Professor?"

"What?"

"How do you find anything?" Logan asked. He almost cringed, knowing that Perry would see the question as yet another indication of what he perceived to be Logan's sadly below average intelligence quotient. "I don't understand your system. Is it computerized?"

Perry mumbled something under his breath that sounded suspiciously like "Moron." He turned away, obviously expecting Logan to follow. "I keep all that information right here, boy," he said, tapping the side of his shiny pate. "I don't need any fancy computer programs."

"But...there must be thousands of artifacts down here!"

"Hundreds of thousands. Most of which have been down here so long that they've been forgotten by everyone but me," Perry said. Logan could swear he detected a sorrowful note in Perry's voice, but decided he must have been imagining things. No pernicious old goat like Perry could possibly be sentimental about anything.

Up and down the rows they wandered, Perry grumbling to himself every step of the way, while Logan followed behind. Eventually, they came to the far side of the basement. Perry stopped, pointing to an unmarked door.

"See this door?" he asked, as if Logan was not standing two feet in front of it.

"Yes, sir."

"Don't ever open it. Ever. Opening this door means instant termination. Understand?"

"What's-"

"Do you understand?" Perry snarled, jabbing a bony finger into Logan's chest.

"Yes, sir. I understand." Good God, the man was a raving lunatic! Logan was seriously beginning to doubt the wisdom in taking the position as Perry's assistant. No wonder it had still been available. No one else was stupid enough to want it.

Perry turned away in a huff, heading toward another door.

"Dr. Perry, what will my responsibilities be?" Logan asked, half expecting Perry to tell him that he was to be Chief Idiot and Ass-kisser.

Perry sighed, as if Logan's question was a huge imposition. "You'll fetch new acquisitions from upstairs, bring 'em down here. You'll make my coffee, which I take black. You'll dust. And most of all, you'll stay the hell out of my way," Perry answered. He walked into his office, a small, dark cubby that was marked by a dull brass plate engraved with Perry's name, slamming the door shut in Logan's face.

Staring at the scarred oak door, Logan blinked. He wrapped his fingers around the doorknob, ready to burst in and tell Perry exactly what he could do with his assistant's position, but hesitated. He couldn't just quit. He had bills to pay – the rent, the utilities, and it would be nice if he could eat something besides Ramen noodles once in a while. Logan's hand fell to his side, his shoulders slumping dejectedly. Like it or not, he was stuck being Perry's assistant, at least until a better opportunity came along.

Damn it.

Picking up a feather duster, Logan reluctantly began his new job.

Two months later, Logan was still dusting and there didn't seem to be an end in sight.

The more his feather duster whacked across the boxes that were stacked on the shelves and the various larger, shroud-covered pieces that were wedged in around the perimeter of the room, the thicker the layer of dust seemed to grow. It felt as if he lived in a perpetual cloud of grime, dust motes coloring his hair and clothes a whitish-gray. His eyes were always itchy and watery, and his nose ran like a leaky faucet. He virtually lived on over-the-counter allergy medications.

During the entire time he'd been there he'd barely heard a word from Perry - just a shout now and then for fresh coffee, or an order to run up to the main floor to pick up a waiting artifact (always accompanied by the obligatory growled warning not to drop it). Without exception, Perry examined, packaged, and labeled the artifacts by himself, leaving Logan the dubious honor of finding some place in the crammed shelves to stick them.

Where Logan would have liked to stick them was directly up Perry's pompous, arrogant ass, and sideways, but he managed – barely - to restrain himself. Even the worst of his college professors, the few who had seemed hell-bent on making certain that Logan never graduated, had not been as surly or condescending as Perry. Now Logan understood why Perry had been relegated to the Museum's dungeons fifty years ago and left there to be as forgotten as half of the artifacts. He was an asshole, plain and simple, and unfit to interact with the surface-dwellers.

That afternoon had been one of the worst since Logan had started his assistant's position with Perry. It began when he brought down a ceramic vase from Acquisitions. It was nothing special – early 20th century, a dime a dozen in any antique store on the East coast. Donated to the museum by a wealthy, if eccentric, patron, Acquisitions had taken one look at it and had condemned it to spend eternity in the dungeons. Not only was it common, it had a hairline crack that ran its length.

Logan dutifully carried it down to the basement and presented it to Perry.

That's when the real trouble started.

"You idiot! I assign you on one simple task, something a five year old could accomplish, and what happens? You crack a valuable vase! An irreplaceable artifact!" Perry said, waving the vase in Logan's face.

"But, Dr. Perry...it's a mass-produced-"

"But? But, nothing! Do you think you can lecture me on what is valuable and what isn't? Do you have fifty years of experience with priceless artifacts? Do you have a Ph.D. in anthropology? No. You have a degree that's one step up from a mail-order diploma, and the brain pan of a gecko!

Within seconds Perry's diatribe rocketed into a full-fledged tantrum, screaming at Logan at the top of his lungs, using every euphemism for stupid known to modern man, and a half dozen more in ancient Latin and Greek.

"I knew I should never have taken on such a dimwitted, irresponsible, moronic half-wit like you! What was I thinking? I told them I didn't need an assistant. Told them that the new generations being spit out by universities today were lazy and careless, but did they listen? No, they did not. You're getting on in years, Perry. You shouldn't be climbing those ladders, Perry. You need to train someone to take over after you retire at the end of the year, Perry. Now look at what you've done!" Perry's face grew red as he ranted, the veins in his temple throbbing visibly. "Idiot! Fool! Imbecile!"

For ten full minutes Perry railed against Logan, until he finally ran out of both steam and insults. With a final nonsensical order for Logan to mop every inch of the concrete floor until it was clean enough to eat off of, Perry huffed and puffed, grabbed his coat and briefcase and left, leaving Logan standing shell-shocked in his wake.

Well, that explained a lot. Not that it excused his behavior, not by a long shot, but it did explain why Perry was behaving like such a shit toward Logan. He was being forced to retire, and evidently Logan was next in line to be crowned Dungeon Master.

Logan leaned back against the wall, looking at the crowded basement with new eyes. Organize. Computerize. Optimize. Get rid of everything that had little or no historic value. Donate it or loan it out to lesser museums. In his mind's eye, Logan saw the dungeon transformed into a newer, brighter, more efficient storage facility. Yes, when he was promoted to Curator of Relics, there would be vast changes made. He'd bring the Museum's dungeons kicking and screaming into the twenty-first century.

His eyes wandered across the room to the Vault, as he'd come to think of the one room in the dungeon that Perry had forbidden him from entering. If he were going to be the new Curator, he should know what was in that room. He should. Really. It only made sense. He should take a peek, just to see what Perry was hiding in there.

Maybe it was something illegal, like black market fossils, or jewels. Logan certainly wouldn't put it past Perry to hoard valuables, especially if they were ill-gotten gains.

Logan's curiosity got the better of him. Perry wouldn't be back for a while, if at all. He had time to take a gander at what lay behind Door Number One without getting caught. Logan walked over to the Vault, eyeing the door warily, as if it might bite him if he tried to open it. It was identical to the one that guarded Perry's office. A small latex glove dispenser was affixed to the wall on one side. There were no markings, nothing to tell Logan what might lay behind it. Worriedly, he looked for wires and contacts that might indicate that the door was alarmed.

"Stop being silly. Perry's got you afraid of your own fucking shadow!" Logan admonished himself. "It's just a door, like any other door in this basement." He took a deep breath to steady his nerves, then used a credit card to jimmy the old-fashioned lock.

The door creaked open with only a slight push from Logan. Feeling along the wall, he found the light switch and flipped it on. A single, naked, low watt bulb suspended from the ceiling on a thin wire flickered to life, casting the room in a weak, yellowish light.

Logan blinked, taking a moment to allow his eyes to adjust to the near dark. Peering in, they widened at what Perry had been keeping hidden in the room.

It was a sarcophagus.

Twelve feet long and four feet deep, covered in at least two inches of dust, it filled the small room nearly from one end to the other.

Logan ran out of the Vault, returning a moment later with an anthropologist's field kit. Carefully, he used a small whisk to brush the thick dust from the lid of the sarcophagus, revealing a life-sized, incredibly realistic effigy.

It had been sculpted entirely in gold. At some point in the recent past someone must have taken great pains to restore it, because there wasn't a single trace of the patina of age anywhere on its magnificent exterior. The warm glow of the gold gleamed, even in the dim light of the Vault.

What the hell was Perry thinking, hiding this wonder down here in the basement? Maybe it's a fake, Logan wondered as he ran his gloved fingers reverently over the sleek, golden effigy. Well, if it is a counterfeit, it's the cleverest, most painstakingly authentic replica I've ever seen.

It was Egyptian, if Logan wasn't mistaken. The man who had been immortalized in gold must have been a high-ranking official, Logan thought absently, to warrant such a coffin. A chieftain, perhaps even a king.

If the effigy was truly representative of the man buried within the sarcophagus, then he had been strikingly handsome when alive. He had had a high forehead, sharply defined cheekbones, and wide-spaced eyes. His nose had been straight, narrow at the bridge; his lips had been perfectly bowed and sensuously full.

The details of the effigy were amazing. Even the man's long braids had been captured in fine gold. Naked, he was obviously male since the sculptor had carved his flaccid, yet impressive, penis in meticulous detail. Broad shoulders, narrow waist and hips, strong thighs and calves – this man must have been a warrior-king, Logan decided. His only adornment was a wide, bejeweled torc at his throat, and an intricately scrolled band that encircled his right bicep.

"Who were you?" Logan whispered. He'd come to the conclusion that the sarcophagus was authentic, if for no other reason than the fact that Perry had kept it locked up in the Vault and had not relegated it to one of the corners of the basement.

Now Logan's blood sang with curiosity. A strange compulsion swept through him, making his heart race.

He wanted to know. Needed to know if the sarcophagus contained a mummy, and if that mummy was the man represented in effigy on the lid.

Perry would never tell him. Perry would go ballistic if he ever found out that Logan had even been inside the Vault. It would be the last straw – Perry would find some-way to get Logan fired.

But he had to know. Logan's chest tightened painfully at the very thought of leaving the Vault without satisfying his curiosity. His lungs wouldn't work; he couldn't draw in a deep breath. Repercussions be damned - he had to know.

And there was only one way Logan could find out.

He needed to open it.

CHAPTER THREE

Feeling instant relief at his decision, and the thrill of discovery coursing through his veins, Logan ran out of the Vault. He returned a few moments later with a heavy black crowbar. Carefully wedging the flat tip under the edge of the lid, he pushed and pried until the lid began to move.

A musty smell of earth and age floated up from the dark recesses of the sarcophagus. Logan slid the heavy lid over until it balanced precariously to one side, and the light of the twenty-first century hit the remains of a man who'd lived millennia ago. Remarkably well preserved, the mummy lay on his back with his arms crossed over his chest. Time and the mummification process had tanned his skin to dark leather, still bearing delicate strips of decayed, gray linen wrappings.

There were no other items in the sarcophagus except for a small jar that rested at the mummy's feet. Frowning, Logan gingerly picked it up, examining it with a studied eye. It was a canopic jar, used by ancient Egyptians to store the internal organs removed during mummification.

Logan knew that according to the belief at the time, a man would have need of all of his body parts on the other side. His internal organs were removed during the mummification process and stored in small jars so that they would be accessible to him in the afterlife.

But this jar was unlike any other Logan had ever seen. That there was only one jar was unusual enough. There were usually four, each bearing the head of a different god. Representing the four sons of the great god, Horus, each godhead guarded a specific organ of the body. Imsety, depicted by a human head, held the liver. Hapi, pictured with the head of a baboon, held the lungs. Finally, there were Duamutef, the jackal, who held the stomach, and Qebehsenuef, depicted with a falcon's head, who held the intestines.

This particular canopic jar had the head of a crocodile. "Setekh," Logan whispered, shaking his head. Why would they put Setekh on a canopic jar? He was the god of storms and disorder, not usually associated with the afterlife. What part of the body did they stick in here? Where are the other jars? Logan's mind sped ahead, trying to reason it out. It can't be the brains - they were always scrambled and discarded. I just don't get it.

He paused as a chill rippled through him and he recalled Jason's words from the bar a couple of months ago. He'd mentioned a giant with a crocodilian head. No, that's rubbish, Logan thought, coincidence, nothing more.

Logan turned the jar around in his hands, examining it from every angle. Carved from a pale rose alabaster, it was a beautiful example of ancient workmanship, for all its unorthodox features. A thin gold seal wrapped around the throat of the jar was inscribed with a series of tiny hieroglyphics. Logan ran his fingers over it, feeling the texture, admiring the delicate lines of the hieroglyphic carvings.

Cursed is he who has no heart

He narrowed his eyes, trying to decipher the inscribed markings. Damn, he really should have paid more attention during his Intro to Egyptian Hieroglyphics class. "Cursed is he who has no heart," Logan haltingly interpreted. "That's odd. He must have been a really bad boy to have been cursed to suffer eternity without a heart."

From his studies in Egyptology, Logan knew that the ancients believed that the heart was the center of intelligence, not the brain. During mummification, the heart was the only organ to be left inside the body, done so that the deceased would be cognizant in the afterlife.

"You will meet a man with no heart."

The chill suddenly returned to touch Logan's spine with a cold finger of foreboding as Jason's words again echoed in his mind. Reflexively, Logan's fingers tightened around the jar.

Suddenly, there was a soft cracking sound as the seal separated, the head of Setekh falling off. As Logan snatched at the free-falling head, his other hand inadvertently tipped the body of the jar toward the sarcophagus. A thin trickle of gritty ash poured out, dusting the mummy's chest a whitish-gray.

"Oh, shit," he whispered, feeling his blood drain into his feet, peering into the empty jar. "I am so screwed. If Perry opens this thing, I won't be able to get a day pass into the museum, never mind work here."

Logan shook as he replaced Setekh's head onto the jar and laid it at the mummy's feet before shoving the heavy sarcophagus lid back into place. He backed out of the Vault's door, closing and locking it behind him. His heart was pounding as he leaned his head against the cool wood.

With any luck, Perry would never know that Logan had trespassed into the Vault, and Logan's secret faux pas would be as forgotten as the mummy itself.

***

In the absolute blackness of the Vault, within the recently disturbed golden tomb, something began to stir.

The ashes of a heart that had been turned to dust centuries ago sank into the hollowed chest cavity of the mummy like sand through a sieve, settling under the breastbone.

It began as a soft, dry rustling sound, like the crinkling of old, brittle parchment. Swiftly, it grew louder, popping and fizzing as if the contents of the sarcophagus were coming to a boil. Wet, slick sounds were accompanied by thuds and bangs as bones, muscles, and cartilage solidified and taut, youthful skin grew to cover them. Joints groaned as they bent for the first time in five millennia.

Dark eyes blinked open, glowing with rage and indescribable pain.

The sarcophagus rocked as its prisoner furiously threw his growing weight against the sides.

As the mummy's larynx rejuvenated, tongue and palate firming, lips refashioning themselves over teeth that rapidly grew white and strong; as lungs inflated and drew in their first breath in thousands of years, Seti screamed.

Logan tried to occupy himself, to keep his mind off of what lay behind the oak door of the Vault, but it wasn't working. He picked up his mop, slopping the wet, stringy tangle of its head across the floor, but no matter how busy he kept his hands, his mind kept returning to the mysterious sarcophagus.

The very existence of the golden tomb in the locked Vault was an enigma. Its value must be incalculable – if it was genuine, the gold itself would have worth beyond measure. Scientifically, even if the mummy was of no consequence to Egyptian history, or if it was indeed only a reproduction – which Logan didn't believe for an instant – the sheer beauty and workmanship of the tomb would have rendered it priceless to a collector.

Logan couldn't figure out why the Museum was hiding such a treasure down in the bowels of the building. Why wasn't it on display? Could it possibly be stolen? Secured on the black market? He didn't think the Museum would risk the consequences of dealing with the fossil-and-artifact underworld, especially since Logan couldn't see the benefit in securing a piece that couldn't be displayed. But, he conceded, it was possible.

Then it occurred to Logan that perhaps the Museum board wasn't aware of the sarcophagus' existence at all. Perhaps Perry had acquired it, squirreling it away behind locked doors. He was sufficiently eccentric and egotistical to stoop low enough to purchase hot relics. Maybe it was to be his retirement fund.

That would explain why Perry guarded the Vault and its contents so zealously. But how did he plan on selling it? The same way he'd bought it, Logan presumed, answering his own question. Perry couldn't simply put it up on eBay. He would have to unload it on the black market.

Logan's mind reeled with questions. How many years had the sarcophagus sat in the dark of the Vault, forgotten by everyone except Perry? More than a handful – it had been thickly covered in dust. More important than where it had come from was the question: who had the mummy been in life? A priest? A king? How had he died? Why had he been buried with a canopic jar bearing the likeness of Setekh? What had happened to the other canopic jars that should have been buried with him?

Logan was sweeping the mop in lazy, preoccupied

circles across the floor, lost in thought, when suddenly a piercing scream shattered the silence of the Dungeon, freezing Logan's blood and nearly bursting his eardrums. The mop clattered to the floor as he dropped it, instinctively covering his ears.

A tremendous boom thundered behind him. A tremor ran under Logan's feet, and he spun around just in time to see a deep, wide crack zigzag through the wood of the heavy oak door of the Vault an instant before it splintered apart like matchsticks.

Standing framed in the shattered remnants of the doorway was a man.

Powerful legs spread wide, his sinewy arms braced against the fractured jamb, his broad shoulders nearly brushed the width of the doorway. Golden brown skin, the color of toffee and as smooth as silk, stretched tightly over muscles that bulged with strength. A golden torc studded with colorful gems encircled his neck, and a scrolled silver armband was wrapped around his right bicep. Other than those two adornments, he was completely naked.

Between his strong, sculpted thighs, his uncut, flaccid penis and furred sac gave mute testament to his sex, should there be any question not addressed by the rest of him.

Long, black braids cascaded over his wide shoulders, falling across his chest and brushing past nipples that were the color of amber gemstones. The beaded tips tickled at the ropy muscles that divided his stomach.

His smooth, dark eyebrows shadowed eyes that were as black as pitch, but glowed with an intensity that staggered Logan as they looked at him from under thick lashes.

Logan felt himself begin to tremble as icy cold droplets of fear trickled down the center of his back. He knew that handsome face. He'd seen it only a short while before – cast in gold on the lid of the sarcophagus.

Suddenly, with a low moan, the man's legs shook and he fell to his knees, his hands sliding down the door frame, fingers digging into the jamb. Logan realized that they were all that held the man up. He was shaking, worse even than Logan.

Logan's feet paid no attention to the warning being shouted in his head. Instead, they propelled him forward, to the stranger's side. Logan crouched down next to him and insinuated a shoulder under the man's arm, bearing a good portion of his substantial weight, helping him stand.

The larger man's weight staggered Logan as he led the man to a shrouded chair. With his free hand, Logan ripped the protective sheet off the Queen Anne chair so that the man could sit down.

The man collapsed into the chair, slumping to one side, breathing hard. Those dark, flashing eyes never left Logan's, nor could Logan break contact with them. It was as if he was spellbound, unable to look away.

"Was it you who freed me?" The man's voice was raspy, and he winced as if speaking was painful. His accent was unlike any Logan had heard before, although his words were clear.

Logan answered with a barrage of questions of his own. "Who are you? How did you get into that room? Is there some sort of secret passageway in there? Where the hell are your clothes?"

"I am Seti."

"Yeah? Okay, Seti. You sit right here. I'm going to call security."

"Summon no one." The command in Seti's voice was so strong that Logan froze, his feet rooted to the floor. His mind screamed at him to run to the nearest phone and dial 911, but his body wouldn't obey his brain's command. "What is your name?"

"Logan. Who are you?" he asked again.

"I have told you my name. Do you not know of me?"

"No, should I?"

"I am Seti!"

"So you said before. And that should mean what to me, exactly?"

Seti's face slackened, as if hit with a terrible truth. "You truly do not know of me?" He tipped his face upward, shouting at the ceiling. "Damn you, Whore of Horus! Was imprisoning me not enough? Did you need to wipe the memory of me from the face of the earth as well?" He shot Logan a sharp look. "If you know not of me, then how then did you know what was needed to free me?"

"Free you? Pal, I don't know what loony bin you broke out of, but I assure you that I had nothing to do with you escaping whatever rubber room they had you locked up in. This is the National Museum of Natural History. I'm Assistant to the Curator of Relics, and you've just destroyed some very valuable private property!" Logan replied with a lot more confidence than he felt, jerking his thumb toward the shattered remains of the door to the Vault. "Did you touch that sarcophagus? Man, if you so much as scratched it, you are in for a world of trouble with Dr. Perry-"

"SILENCE! You jabber like a tent full of old women." Seti tipped his head from side to side, cracking his neck. In the silence of the basement, each pop sounded like a gunshot. "Where is this National Museum that you say I have found myself in?"

"The moon," Logan said, sarcastically. Who the hell did this guy think he was, anyway? "This is a restricted area of the Museum. You must have set off a half dozen alarms when you broke in here. The police are probably already on their way."

Seti fired Logan a look that made Logan think twice about his flippant answer. "Listen to me very carefully," he said, his black eyes snapping with anger. "I have spent the last five thousand years in a box, unable to move, unable to speak, but fully aware of the passing of time. I could hear everything that went on around me. That was the worse part of my curse. The awareness. But it is how I learned to speak your language. It is also how I know what the moon is, and why this Museum could not possibly be on it. Do not lie to me again."

Logan swallowed hard. Not that he believed the crazy part about Seti being in a box for five millennia, but because there was something in Seti's eyes that belied the sternness in his voice. For all of Seti's posturing, for all his size and obvious strength, the man was afraid and that struck a chord in Logan's heart. He felt sorry for the poor nut.

"Look, if you hurry you can probably make it out of the Museum before the cops get here-"

"The police are not coming, Logan. I did not set off any alarms, because I did not break in. I was already in here," Seti said. His shoulders slumped and he sighed deeply. "In the sarcophagus. My tomb."

"Your tomb? So, you're telling me that...what?" That you're the mummy?" Logan smirked. "Please. Do I look like I fell off the turnip truck yesterday?"

"You do not look like you've been injured recently, no," Seti replied, looking Logan over. Logan could feel those ebony eyes ghosting over his body no less than if Seti's fingers had touched him. He shivered as Seti's sloe eyes awoke parts of Logan that were better left sleeping.

Something wicked sparked in Seti's eyes as they met Logan's, a hot ember that flared for an instant, one that matched the fire that had been kindled in Logan's core.

Then it was gone, replaced by the same mask of cool conceit Seti had worn since he'd first begun to speak.

"Go look," he ordered in a smug voice. "See for yourself, so that you will not again doubt my words."

"This is ridiculous," Logan murmured. Yet he felt a sudden, strong, irresistible urge to do just as Seti had ordered. Before he knew it his feet were moving toward the Vault. His muscles bunched as his body fought itself, his brain issuing stern commands to stop, but his legs paying absolutely no attention.

Logan reached the Vault and, taking a deep breath to collect his frazzled nerves, peered inside.

CHAPTER FOUR

The Vault was better lit than it had been the first time Logan had opened it, even without flipping on the light switch, thanks to the gaping hole Seti had made in the door. Bright light from the main room streamed in, glinting off the golden sarcophagus.

The lid had been tossed to the side, landing end up against one of the walls. A spider web of long, jagged cracks laced through the golden effigy, heaviest at the head where they obscured the sculpted face.

One look told Logan that the sarcophagus was empty. Nevertheless, Logan ducked into the room, first peering carefully into the empty tomb then into all the shadowed corners. He crawled behind the sarcophagus, checking every inch of the floor, looking for the mummy. He banged on the walls, listening for any hollow echo that might indicate a hidden doorway or passage.

But there was no trace of the mummy anywhere, and no way that Logan could find for it to have been spirited out. For that matter, there was no way he could find for Seti to have gotten into the locked room except through the door he had shattered. It was as if the mummy had vanished into thin air. That unbelievable but undeniable observation posed a problem for Logan's pragmatic mind.

Logan was a scientist, a researcher. Methodical, unlikely to jump to conclusions, he had been trained to carefully study the evidence long and hard before posing an hypothesis. In this case, however, the facts spoke loud and clear – the mummy was gone.

Poof.

The facts were irrefutable, and the conclusion Logan began to draw - however outlandish - seemed the only valid explanation for the series of events.

Fact: The mummy had been locked behind a closed door, safely sealed within its golden tomb. Logan had seen it with his own eyes, had locked the door himself.

Fact: In the next moment it had vanished like an assistant in a magic act. Unlike said assistant, however, the mummy hadn't fallen through a trap door, or scuttled off behind a curtain. Logan had thoroughly checked the floor and walls for any sign of a hidden entrance, and had found none. Nothing. Nada. Zip. Just solid, immoveable concrete block walls and a poured cement floor.

Fact: A man had appeared in the very same closed, locked room, as naked as the mummy had been, and bearing a startling resemblance to the effigy sculpted on the lid of the sarcophagus.

Conclusion A: Seti was a member of a subversive, futuristic nudist society and had been beamed inside the room at the same time the mummy had been beamed out by way of some top-secret, highly questionable, utterly improbable transporting device.

Conclusion B: The man who called himself Seti was the mummy, just as he purported himself to be. He looked like the golden effigy because he had been the model the artist had used to render it.

Occam's Razor, Logan thought. "Entia non sunt multiplicanda praeter necessitatem," which translated stated, "entities should not be multiplied beyond necessity." In other words, all things being equal, the simplest solution tends to be the correct one.

Seti, the naked man who had a face and body that could make the angels weep at its beauty and who was sitting not twenty feet away from Logan, was…

"…a five thousand year old dead guy," Logan whispered in awe.

Logan felt himself begin to shake as he stepped outside of the Vault and stared hard at Seti, not certain at all how to handle the subject of his newly formed hypothesis. On one hand, if it was true then Seti possessed a wealth of first-hand knowledge that would be invaluable to the scientific community. Simply put, he was a history-geek's wet dream. On the other hand, he was a walking corpse who had last seen the light of day before the birth of the pyramids.

He didn't look like a corpse. In fact, he looked like one of the men who graced the covers of the skin magazines that were stacked in Logan's bottom dresser drawer at home. The kind that had inspired one-handed orgasms over the years – tall, handsome, with a hard, sculpted body.

Seti was still slumped in the Queen Anne chair where Logan had left him, looking drained and worn-out. No wonder. Rejuvenating from a state that was only one step up from dust must have been exhausting.

"Now do you believe?" Seti's voice sounded as weary as he looked.

"Maybe," Logan hedged. Saying out it out loud was a step Logan wasn't yet prepared to take. "You need to understand how impossible this all seems."

"Impossible?" Seti sniffed. "Nothing is impossible where the gods are concerned."

"God did this to you?"

"No, your Jehovah had nothing to do with this. At the time I was cursed he had not yet made his presence known in the pantheon of the Immortals. It was Setekh," Seti said, venomously. "Demon bastard of a mongrel's whore." There was obviously no love lost between Seti and the god whose name he bore.

"Setekh cursed you? That's why the canopic jar bore the head of a crocodile! I was right. It was meant to represent Setekh!" Logan couldn't keep the excitement out of his voice as his deduction was validated. He'd thought that the jar symbolized Set, although he hadn't known why. "But you were mummified. What happened to the other canopic jars?"

"Must we have this conversation now?" Seti growled. "I am hungry, thirsty, and grow impatient with your questions."

"Look, Boris Karloff, I think I'm entitled to a few answers," Logan said, sarcastically. "I was living in a nice, safe, rational world up until a few minutes ago. If you're going to expect me to believe that you are who you say you are, then I think I deserve a few details."

"I will tell you all you wish to know after we leave this place."

"Leave? Where do you think you're going to go? You can't run around New York in nothing but your skin. People don't do that anymore. We're civilized now."

"Civilized? How is covering yourselves with cloth from neck to ankle when it is not needed for protection from the elements a mark of progress? It seems idiotic to me, as if your people wish to keep secret the fact that they have genitals."

Logan blinked. "Point taken, but you still can't do it. You'd be arrested before you got ten feet from the building."

Seti rolled his eyes. "As you wish. Secure clothing for

me if you must, but hurry. I wish to shake the dust of this place from my feet as soon as possible."

"Do I look like your personal valet?"

"My apologies," Seti replied sarcastically. "We will sit here until your Dr. Perry returns. Then you can explain to him how his precious sarcophagus was destroyed, and that the naked man is, in fact, the mummy he has so jealously guarded these past fifty years."

Logan opened his mouth to retort, but closed it again with an audible clack. His head swiveled, looking back and forth between Seti, sitting regally before him in all of his naked glory, and the ruins of the Vault.

Shit. Seti is right. Perry will never believe me. One look at the mess in the basement and Perry will have me spitted and roasting in courtroom hell. Breaking and entering. Vandalism. Grand Theft. The possible charges loomed up before Logan's eyes in big, flaming red letters. He could already hear the prison cell door slamming shut and his life as a free citizen saying goodbye for the next ten or twenty years.

"Wait here," Logan ordered, pointing a finger at Seti. "Don't move, and don't touch anything. I'll be right back." Before Seti could say a word to the contrary, Logan raced off.

He took the stairs two at a time, not wanting to waste a moment waiting for an elevator that was notoriously slow and cranky. Logan flew up the four flights of stairs, reaching the Lobby level of the Museum out of breath, but in record time.

He threaded his way against the flow of the steady stream of visitors, entering the Museum gift shop. Logan grabbed a black t-shirt that read, appropriately enough, "The Dead Come Alive at the National Museum of Natural History," and a pair of matching sweat pants with the logo of the Museum embroidered at the hip. A pair of flip-flops completed his purchase, which he charged to the last of his charge cards that miraculously still had credit available. He grabbed the clothing from the cashier without waiting for either a receipt or a bag, returning to the basement praying that Seti had listened and was still there waiting for him.

He was, although he looked less than happy about having been made to wait. His dark chocolate eyes narrowed as Logan approached, and the air took on a decidedly frosty chill.

Tough titties, Logan thought. This superiority thing Seti had going was starting to get on Logan's nerves. He thrust the shirt, pants, and sandals at Seti with a barked order to get dressed. "Hurry up," he said. "I've got to get you out of here before Perry comes back."

Seti stared at the clothes in his hands as if he'd never seen such things before. With a start, Logan realized that he probably hadn't. All facts pointed to Seti having spent the last five thousand years in a box, Logan reminded himself. "I could hear everything that went on around me," Seti had said. Hear, but not see.

Logan sighed, reaching for the t-shirt. "Let me help you," he offered, fitting the shirt over Seti's head. "Your arms go in the smaller holes."

Within a few moments, Seti was dressed, looking like any one of a thousand tourists who visited the Museum each week. Except that Seti's phenomenal body made the cheap t-shirt and sweat pants look as good as if they were tailored Armani. He wore them with grace and ease, as if he'd been born to them.

Damn it. Logan realized that he could dress Seti in a potato sack and the man would still look like a million bucks. He was going to draw attention, like it or not.

"All right. Stay close to me, don't wander off, don't make eye contact, and for the love of God, don't speak with anyone!" Logan growled.

He had no idea where he could possibly take Seti and not be found within the first five minutes. All he knew was that they couldn't stay in the Museum.

Logan led Seti out of the Dungeon and up the stairs that led to the main floor, making a beeline for the exit. The Museum was crowded, as was usual for late afternoon, and walking against the crowd slowed them down considerably. They'd only gone about fifty yards when Logan turned around to make sure that Seti was keeping close behind him.

He wasn't.

It took a full five minutes for Logan to backtrack, finding Seti standing in the Hall of Mammals, staring nostalgically at a stuffed camel.

A trio of women spotted him almost at the same time, zeroing in on Seti like a group of heat-seeking missiles. They whispered to each other as they approached Seti, and Logan held no doubts as to the topic of their conversation. The subject was Seti and the question was how long it would take them to get him out of his new t-shirt and sweatpants.

Logan sprinted back, grabbing Seti's arm and tugging hard, to the annoyance of the three women, who had evidently just declared Seti their own personal museum souvenir. The women practically snarled at Logan as he dragged a reluctant Seti away from the exhibit and back toward the exit.

"I told you to stay behind me!" he hissed, as Seti shook off his arm.

"You are not the master here."

"Oh, and I suppose you are?"

"I am Seti. It is my birthright to rule."

"Yeah? Well, I'm Logan, and it's my right to kick your sorry ass if you do that again!"

"How can my posterior be apologetic for anything?" Seti scoffed. "Besides, with those short stumpy legs of yours, I doubt that you could kick high enough to reach it."

"My legs are not stumpy!" Logan retorted before he saw the flash of humor in Seti's eyes. Great. The dead guy was being witty. "Oh, very funny. Look, just stay with me, okay? The sooner we get out of here, the better off we'll both be."

A security guard stood sentry at the exit turnstiles. Just as they approached him, his radio crackled to life.

Heavy static slurred the voice, and the guard played with the knobs on his radio unit, trying for better reception. The voice could have been asking the guard what he wanted for dinner, but Logan was too nervous to realize that. In his mind, Perry had found the empty sarcophagus and was issuing an all points bulletin for Logan.

"Oh, shit!" Logan whispered. "They couldn't have found the Vault so soon! Damn it, I didn't expect Perry to be back for hours yet! Come on, we've got to get out of here!" He stepped up the pace, walking as quickly as he could without actually breaking into a run.

Luckily for Logan, the security guard didn't look twice at either him or Seti. He was too busy playing with the buttons on his radio to notice the two men who zipped past him and out of the building, disappearing into the crowds on the street.

CHAPTER FIVE

S eti stopped along the street every five feet despite Logan's protests, gawking at one thing or another. He couldn't help himself. It had been so long since he'd last seen anything but the inside of the lid of his sarcophagus, that the sights, sounds, and smells of the city overwhelmed him. And never, even when he'd been alive, traveling the land with his people, had he seen such a conglomeration of oddities.

Perry had spent countless hours over the years speaking to him as he lay immobile in his sarcophagus, instructing him on what changes time had wrought on the world. Seti had come to understand that cities were what people now called their camps. What he hadn't understood was how immense, how unbelievably vast, those cities might be, nor how crowded with human life.

Where on Ra's green earth did all of these people come from? He hadn't known that the world could hold so many, let alone all in one place.

People of all different sizes, shapes, and colors, male and female, old and young, strolled or hurried along. The streets teemed with them. Seti couldn't differentiate between classes, either. Few people had facial markings, but there were many with colorful tattoos. Some wore jewelry and other marks of status, but others around them didn't behave as if those marked were of a higher or lower rank than they. As improbable as it sounded, it seemed that all classes of people here mixed freely with one another, with none showing deference to the other. How odd.

Most people were dressed in garments similar to those Logan had procured for him, but a few wore considerably less. Some so much so that Seti would have wondered why they had bothered with clothing at all, if Logan had not already told him of the ridiculous edicts about public nudity.

And the buildings! So tall that their roofs disappeared into the clouds, they looked as if they'd been hewn from solid rock. He ran his fingers over the smooth, cold surface of the cornerstone of one such wonder, marveling at the workmanship of the perfectly square stone. Amazing.

But what captured Seti's imagination like nothing else were the automobiles. Oh, he'd heard Perry talking about them, and had understood that they were some kind of miraculous conveyance, but to actually see them moving up and down the streets without a single horse or camel in sight was unsettling. If he didn't know better, he would have thought them the work of some god.

A young woman with hair so bright a red that it looked aflame sold what she called deeveedees from a battered suitcase on the curb. Before Logan could stop him, Seti grabbed one of the thin boxes that she had on display, cracking it open. Disappointingly, the deeveedees were no more than small, flat metal discs that served no obvious purpose that Seti could fathom. Perhaps they were weapons of some sort, he reasoned. Logan jerked it out of his hand before Seti could test his theory.

Mouthwatering aromas drew him next to a small metal cart where a man peddled twisted pieces of bread sprinkled generously with salt. In Seti's day, salt had been a precious commodity, readily available only near the sea or from a few scattered and rare salt licks, and he was duly impressed by the merchant's wealth. The smell of the baked bread made his stomach grumble, reminding him that he was famished.

"I need food," he told Logan, fully expecting to be obeyed immediately. Unfortunately, Logan was proving to be frustratingly disobedient. He hadn't obeyed a direct order from Seti yet.

"In a while. We have to keep moving!" Logan replied, tugging at his arm.

"Now."

"Later!"

Obstinate servant! Seti wondered how the kings of this modern world kept their servants in line, since he saw no evidence of lashings on any of the people around him. Obviously, whatever their method, Seti was doing it wrong. Logan fought him at every turn.

Logan's hand was tugging incessantly on his arm again. Seti allowed himself to be pulled along the sidewalk, but only until the next wonder caught his eye. Seti planted his feet and it would have taken a man much larger and stronger than Logan to budge him.

Window glass amazed him. It was nothing like Seti had imagined it to be. A most interesting invention, he thought, tapping his fingers against the storefront pane. Nearly invisible, hard, it let abundant light into the shop. Still, Seti considered, it also allowed prying eyes to see into a man's personal affairs, just as Seti was doing now. He watched a young man slip curious-looking sandals on the feet of several patrons who sat within the shop. How did these people tolerate strangers nosing about in their business? Seti would never stand for anyone gawking at him.

Everywhere he looked, sights, sounds, and smells both alien and fascinating assaulted him, intriguing and beguiling him. Most were benign, some were enchanting – like the pretzel, as Logan had called the small, twisted loaves of bread – but some were completely repugnant.

Such a repulsive smell wafted to his nose at that moment, drifting up from a circular hole in the road. Seti winced, recoiling from the stench.

"Must be a sewer break," Logan muttered, wrinkling his nose and tugging yet again on Seti's arm.

Thank the gods, that smell must not be common here, Seti thought. Logan finds it as horrendous as I do. For once, Seti was happy to allow Logan to lead him away.

Logan turned into a darkened doorway, dragging Seti behind him. He didn't want to enter – Seti had spent far long enough boxed up in a small, dark place. He wanted to see the sky, feel the fresh air caress his cheek.

But he was also hungry and thirsty, so much so that he was beginning to feel weaker by the minute, and Logan had promised him both food and drink if he came inside. Seti did as Logan bade him but with great reluctance.

He hated having to rely on Logan for his sustenance. It should be the other way around. Seti was a king, therefore the provider. It had always been that way, and it went against his grain to be dependent on anyone.

Still, he had no choice, at least not for now. He followed Logan into the building, through a dimly lit room to a table near the back. Seti slid in over the cracked leather, sitting opposite Logan.

"Well, who do we have here? Where did you find this hunk of fine-looking man flesh, Logan?"

"He's…a friend from out of town, Wendy. On vacation," Logan replied, eyeing Seti. A warning not to divulge his true origins, Seti surmised. Very well. By this point, if it would get him some food and water, Seti would gladly claim to be a lump of dung fresh from a camel's ass.

"What's your name, lover?" Wendy, as Logan had called the old woman, asked him.

"Seti."

"Seti what?"

"Seti...from out of town."

Wendy chuckled. "Cute and a sense of humor. Can't beat that combination, Logan. I think he's a keeper. All right, boys, what'll you have?"

Logan ordered the food – burgers, fries, and a pitcher. Seti had heard of burgers and fries, and had high hopes that the pitcher would contain liquid of some sort.

Having suffered a constant, gnawing ache in his belly for thousands of years, his throat as parched as the desert sands, he nonetheless had survived – in a manner of speaking. And yet within the scant few hours since the curse had been broken, Seti felt as though his strength was draining away, leaving him as weak as an infant. He could barely sit upright. That, he remembered, was the curse of having flesh.

Wendy shuffled off, leaving them alone at their table.

"Okay. I want some answers," Logan said. "Supposing – just supposing, mind you – that I believe you are who you say you are, then why now? Why me? Why didn't you regenerate, or de-mummify, or whatever it is that you did today when your sarcophagus was first opened?"

"My tomb was never opened until now," Seti replied, shrugging his shoulders. "The curse would not allow it. I was doomed to spend five thousand years entombed, and today must mark the last day of my sentence."

"You mean to tell me that this curse kept everyone who came in contact with your sarcophagus from opening it? That's ridiculous!"

"No more ridiculous than you breaking bread with... what did you call me? Oh, yes. The five thousand year old dead guy," Seti countered.

"I remain unconvinced of that fact," Logan said. There was a defiant tilt to his chin that made Seti want to smile. He looked like a small boy stubbornly refusing to obey his parents. "If it's true, then you must know things about history that no one else alive – for lack of a better word – knows. Tell me something about the Renaissance. Something no one else would know."

"I cannot. I know little of history except my own."

"Aha!" Logan cried, jabbing a finger at Seti. "I knew it! You don't know anything because you aren't the mummy!"

"I know little because my tomb was only discovered less than a hundred years ago," Seti replied patiently. "I spent the preceding four thousand nine hundred years buried under a hundred feet of sand."

"You were buried…"

"…alive, for lack of a better term." Seti finished Logan's sentence, watching his face pale as the truth slowly sank in. "In answer to your earlier question, there was only one canopic jar because I do not believe Setekh ever intended for me to live again, either in this world or the next."

Logan sat back in his seat, the air in his lungs escaping in a long, low whoosh. "Jesus, Seti. How did you not lose your mind? Five thousand years…"

Seti smiled softly at the compassion he heard in Logan's voice as the enormity of Seti's curse hit him.

"I spent a great deal of time, especially in the beginning, thinking of Setekh and the countless, creative ways in which I would kill him, had he been human. After that? I slept as often as I could, hoping my dreams would bring to me someone I once knew."

"Ah," Logan whispered. "Your wife. Did you have children, Seti?"

"Thirty-two at last count," His smile was bittersweet, remembering the dozens of dark-headed young ones scampering about his tents. "But I had no wives. Concubines, yes, but I never took any woman as a wife."

"Thirty-two! Then you might have family, Seti! Great-great-whatevers."

Seti chuckled. "Perhaps. Life was harsh then, Logan. There is no telling that any of my blood survived. Or that Setekh allowed them to live after I was gone. In fact, I am certain that he did not. Part of my curse was to be forgotten, and that would include the decimation of my bloodline."

"That's awful. I'm sorry, Seti. For what happened to you. What exactly did happen, by the way? What caused you to be cursed in the first place?"

A dark cloud colored Seti's face as memories assailed him, bidden by Logan's innocent question. Memories he'd spent the last five thousand years trying to forget. "I don't wish to speak of it."

Wendy saved Seti from the myriad of questions he knew danced on the tip of Logan's tongue by setting steaming platters of food in front of them, and a pitcher of something amber and frosty cold between himself and Logan. "Eat up, boys. The pitcher's on me."

"Thanks, Wendy," Logan said, smiling up at her.

"Yes. My thanks," Seti parroted. In his day, servants were never thanked for the service they provided – it was their place, their duty in his world to serve. But it seemed times had changed, as he noticed more and more with every passing moment.

"You're welcome, hon. Make sure Logan eats – he's too skinny," she smiled as she walked away.

Skinny? Logan did not seem underweight to Seti. He was smaller than Seti, certainly, but his flesh seemed firm and his muscles strong. As they ate, Seti seized the opportunity to fully appreciate the young man who had released him.

Logan's light brown hair was cut short, just long enough to curl over the tips of his ears and brush the collar of his shirt. He had a pleasant face, open and honest, and his smile – on the rare occasion that he let it tilt his full lips – was winsome. There was a single dimple that deepened in his left cheek when he allowed himself to grin boyishly.

But it was his eyes that captivated Seti, and had since the moment Seti had awoken and stepped out from the chamber in which his sarcophagus had been kept.

They were large, expressive, intelligent, framed by dark lashes that were so long that they curled.

More than that, Logan's eyes were a bright green. A familiar green; a green that had haunted Seti's sleep for thousands of years.

Impossible, the voice of reason in Seti's head said emphatically. It cannot be. He is no more than the dust of the earth now, dead before Set laid the curse on your head.

And yet...

Stop it. You look for similarities where there are none. Again that irritating inner voice remonstrated.

But how wonderful would it be, how comforting, to have some connection to his past, however fragile. Especially if it was a connection to the only one who had ever held Seti's heart.

Ashai.

The name floated through Seti's mind like a prayer. His throat constricted as memories of Ashai swept through him, unbidden. His laugh, low and free, his gentle touch. His kiss, his body...

Enough!

Seti turned his thoughts back to the food Wendy had placed before him by sheer force of will. So this was a burger, he thought, picking it up. For years he had heard Perry speaking to others, ordering them to fetch him one. He examined it before biting into it. Two round slices of bread enveloped a char-burned piece of meat. It didn't look very appetizing, but it smelled wonderful. Seti's stomach growled angrily, reminding him that he hadn't eaten in millennia.

He opened his mouth wide and took a large bite. Thick and medium rare, the meat's juices ran down his chin, its smoky flavor filling his mouth, his eyes rolling back in his head in delight.

"This is good," he said around a mouthful of beef. "More."

"One is enough for now. That stuff will clog up your arteries," Logan replied, pouring them each a mug of the cold, amber liquid. "Besides, we have to get going soon. It's only a matter of time until the authorities come here, looking for me."

"I will protect you. I will allow no one to harm you."

"Yeah, right. How do you plan on doing that? You don't have any weapons, and even if you did you can't just enter into hand-to-hand combat with the New York City Police Department."

"I am Seti. I have other resources."

"How comforting."

"After all you have seen today, you still doubt me?"

"The only thing I don't doubt is that I've lost my mind."

"Still you scoff. What will it take to convince you that I am who I say I am?"

"At this point it doesn't really matter, Seti. Whether or not you're the mummy or just some fabulously inventive thief, the consequences of taking you out of the museum and not turning you in will be the same for me."

"I will protect you," Seti said again. He grew weary of

the argument, feeling as though he was butting his head against sandstone. "What is this?" he asked, picking up the mug, seeking to change the tiresome subject.

"Beer."

Seti cocked a brow, sniffing at the mug. "What is this white foam?"

"That's the head."

"Your beer is alive?"

"No, that's just what we call the foam."

"It doesn't smell like beer."

"How would you know?"

"We had fine beer in my day. Brewed with barley and wheat," Seti answered. He took a small sip of the golden liquid, immediately crinkling his nose. "This is not beer. This is piss water."

"This draft is Budweiser! That's the King of Beers," Logan protested.

"King? Nonsense. This swill would not be fit for peasants to drink! Beer should have a sweet, fruity taste. Not like this piss."

"Kindly stop calling it piss. Wendy bought us this pitcher – you should be grateful."

"Are you certain that she bought the pitcher and did not simply p-"

"You'll never know how much is riding on you not finishing that sentence," Logan growled.

Seti smiled. Not the weak, half-smiles he'd been allowing himself since his reanimation, but a full, wide, delighted smile. How brave young Logan was, defending his friend, no matter that Seti was bigger and stronger than he. How loyal. In Seti's day such stalwartness would have made Logan a fine warrior, one trusted and admired for his grit, and he told Logan so.

"Warrior? Me? I'm a bookworm, Seti. I spend all of my time either nose-deep in textbooks or up to my armpits in old, dead things."

"Old, dead things like me?" Seti chuckled at the chagrin on Logan's face.

"That's not what I meant," Logan replied, blushing furiously. "I'm no warrior."

"I did not say that you were. I said that you had the makings of one."

"Right now, I'd settle for the makings of the Invisible Man. Hurry and finish, Seti. We have to get out of here."

No sooner had the words left Logan's lips than there was a flurry of activity at the front door of the establishment. Two men hovered near the door, their presence vaguely menacing, obviously looking for someone or something.

For them, Seti realized.

"Oh, shit!" Logan whispered, his face strained and pale. "We're fucked. There's no way we can slip out without them seeing us."

"These men seek to do you harm?"

"They don't look like cops. They might be private security from the Museum. But either way they're going to find us, and we're going to be in for a shitload of trouble. I just know it."

"I will allow no one to harm you. I already told you this."

"You can't stop them, Seti, and there's no way we can get past them," Logan replied, shaking his head. "You don't have a weapon, and I wouldn't want you to use one if you did. That would only get us into worse trouble."

"I also told you that I have other resources."

Seti looked over at the men. One of them was talking with the barkeep, who pointed a finger toward Logan and Seti's table. Seti narrowed his eyes, then closed them, reaching out, calling to the wind.

Would it remember his voice, even after all these years? Or would his command go unheeded?

He needn't have worried.

The wind answered in a howl, smashing open the doors of the bar, blowing in the two large pane glass windows at the front. People fell like dominos, toppled by the fury of the gale, scrambling for cover from the shards of window glass. Like a monstrous entity, the wind swept through the room blowing dishes and glasses off the tables, lifting dust, broken glass, peanut shells, and napkins up into the air.

A funnel swirled to life in the center of the bar, standing as an impenetrable barrier between Seti and Logan and the men who sought them. Screams were heard under the roar of the wind as people fought to escape the terrifying maelstrom that undulated and twisted like a wind-demon, sucking everything that wasn't bolted to the floor into its deadly embrace.

Seti grabbed Logan's wrist, pulling him from his seat and dragging him toward a door at the back of the bar. He could not keep the wind constrained for long. He was still too weak.

A wild-eyed Wendy stood in the doorway, staring at the carnage being created in the bar by the storm. The woman was Logan's friend, Seti reminded himself, even if she did serve piss-water and call it beer. He grabbed her hand, pulling her along with them. There was a door at the back of the kitchen, and Seti dragged them both through it just as he lost his grip on the storm.

The shriek of the wind grew louder, deafening even in the back alley as the storm within the bar exploded. Seti peered into the kitchen, where he could see flashes of lightning coming from the bar as the tempest grew in power, thunder crashing, shaking the very foundations of the building.

They needed to get away. The storm would blow itself out quickly now, and the Museum's men would continue their search for Seti and Logan.

"Where is your home, Logan?" Seti asked. He shook Logan lightly, until at last the fear and confusion drained away from Logan's eyes. "Your home. Where is it?"

"Oh, yeah…we can't go to my place. They'll be watching it, I'm sure," Logan said. "We can go to Jason's apartment."

"What was that?" Wendy interjected, tugging on Seti's arms. Her eyes were still wide with terror and she shook so badly that Seti feared she would collapse.

"Sit down, Wendy. All will be well, now. You are no longer in danger. Listen! The wind dies even as we speak," Seti said distractedly, helping lower her to the ground. He had more pressing matters to tend to than a frightened woman. Seti turned his dark eyes on Logan. "Who is this Jason?" he asked, feeling an unexpected, piercing shaft of jealously slice through him. He shook it off, telling himself that he only cared because he wished no one else to know of his existence.

"He's one of my best friends – we can hide out at his place."

"We must go," Seti said firmly. He didn't like the idea of seeking shelter with this friend of Logan's, but he realized that he had little choice in the matter. He urged Logan into motion, although it was plain that Logan did not want to leave Wendy sitting in the muck of the alleyway. "She will be all right, Logan. We will not be if we do not leave this place."

Logan nodded, squatting down at Wendy's side. "You okay?" he asked, putting his hand on her shoulder.

"Leave her!" Seti ordered, towering over them both, glaring at Logan for disobeying him – yet again.

"I'm not leaving until I'm sure she's okay," Logan

yelled, scowling up at Seti. He turned back to Wendy, whose frightened face was streaked with tears. "Wendy? Are you all right?"

Seti was tempted to pick Logan up and throw him over a shoulder, giving him no choice but to leave, every instinct telling Seti to flee. He wanted – needed - to get Logan to safety, and Logan's refusal to leave was infuriating him.

"Logan!" he roared. "We need to leave!"

"You're in trouble, aren't you, Logan?" Wendy asked, wiping away tears with the back of her hand. "You need to go, kid. I'll be fine," she said, giving a small laugh. "I'm a tough old broad. Listen to your friend. Go. And don't worry…I never saw you today."

"Are you sure?" Logan asked, giving Wendy a hug.

Seti's fingers itched to drag Logan up from the ground by the hair. "Logan!" he hissed, "The storm has ceased. They will be coming!"

"Go on. I'm fine," Wendy said. She looked up at Seti, narrowing her eyes at him. "You take care of this boy, you hear me? Don't let anybody hurt him, Seti. He's like my own son."

"I'm a big boy, Wendy," Logan said. Seti could tell that Wendy's declaration had embarrassed Logan by the blush that crept up his neck. "I can take care of myself."

"Then go, already!" Wendy said, giving Logan a push.

Logan stood up, much to Seti's relief. He grabbed Logan's arm, pulling him bodily down the alley toward the street.

There was a huge crowd gathered outside the bar, voices chattering excitedly about the damage, survivors, bruised and bloody, wandering in shock along the sidewalk. Logan and Seti took advantage of the chaos, melting into the crowd and disappearing.

CHAPTER SIX

"We have a problem," Perry whispered angrily into his old, black rotary phone. His fingers drummed nervously on the desktop as he waiting for a reaction from the other end.

His declaration was met by silence. Then a voice answered him in a clipped, cultured monotone. "You had better have a vital reason for calling me at this number. Any news less than catastrophic will prove detrimental to your health."

"It's gone. Is that cataclysmic enough for you?"

"Gone?" There was a hint of unease in the cultivated voice, a slight wavering of control. "What do you mean, it's gone?"

"Just what I said. The sarcophagus has been destroyed, and the mummy is missing."

"That's ridiculous." The voice dripped with derision. "The curse will not allow anyone to break the seals on the sarcophagus until the very last day of Seti's sentence ends."

"I know the fundamentals of the curse as well as you do, Ethan. Still, the mummy is gone. What does that tell you?"

Silence returned, thick and heavy with unspoken disbelief. "Surely you jest. Must I remind you of how little patience I have? Levity will get you killed, Perry."

"Do I sound as if I'm joking? Your threats mean nothing to me at this point, Ethan," Perry hissed, spittle coating the telephone receiver. "You were wrong! I've asked you repeatedly over the years to let me verify your research-"

"My data was sound, Perry, and my translation was accurate. The curse will be broken in exactly one month from today. You tire me with your incessant worrying."

Perry snorted, a dry, humorless sound. "It appears that your translation is flawed, Ethan. Your dates are off by thirty days. That sarcophagus was broken out of, not into. He's come back, and now he's loose in New York."

"That's impossible!"

"Evidently not. This is what comes of your pretentious, arrogant, supercilious attitude, Ethan. You never trusted any of us with the translations. You had to prove that you were the most brilliant, the most crucial to our cause. You were so afraid that one of us might find an error in your work that-"

"Enough! I didn't waste my time and fortune only to have victory snatched from my hands by a few days! If it's true that Seti has returned, then he couldn't have gotten far. He would have no idea of where he is, of what the world had become in his absence. He'd stick out like a naked thumb on the street. Find him."

"I'm certain that he's with my assistant, Logan-"

"Your assistant? Do you have any idea of what might happen if he talks to anyone about who and what Seti is?" Perry could hear the fury fueled by fear rising in Ethan's voice. His carefully cultured voice became strained and strident. It was almost worth losing Seti just to hear Ethan Wilder lose his composure.

"I've already sent security to find them-"

"Kindly tell me you weren't stupid enough to tell your rent-a-cops anything!"

"Of course not. I may not be the exalted Ethan Wilder, but I'm not an idiot. I told them that my new assistant had stolen a valuable gold torc – the one Seti should be wearing. When they find Logan and Seti, they're to bring them both back to me."

"Everything we've worked for these last fifty years hinges on finding him, Perry. He's an Immortal. The secret to everlasting life runs through his veins. I want that secret, Perry."

"So do I, Ethan."

"Then find him!"

"I will. But I need you to tap into your vast resources. Find out all you can about Logan Ashton, my assistant. Who are his friends? Where is his family? If security comes back without Seti, I need to know where to send them next. I need to know where Logan would go for help."

"I'll get back to you as soon as I get the information. And, Perry? Do not fuck this up. Seti was your responsibility, and I will not let such failure go unpunished."

The phone went dead as the connection was broken, leaving Perry listening to dead air.

Dead, just like Perry himself would be soon enough, if they didn't find Seti. He'd been battling liver disease for years, hoping and praying that it didn't kill him before Seti's awakening.

Fifty years ago, five scientists working on a dig in Egypt had discovered a tomb buried in the sand. No pyramid marked the grave, and yet the sarcophagus had clearly been that of someone of high status. The tomb chamber was an anomaly – its seals had been completely intact with no signs of pilfering by thieves, and yet no artifacts aside from the sarcophagus had been found within it. No utensils or pottery, no riches that normally littered such a site were in evidence. Whoever the mummy had been in life, he had been buried without any of the luxuries he'd left behind.

Strange hieroglyphics had been carved into the base of the sarcophagus, markings that were not easily translated, even with the help of the Rosetta Stone. But Ethan had worked on the translations day and night, and when the meaning had finally become clear it had rocked the team to their cores.

Every one of them was aware of the legend of Seti, the king who had been cursed by his namesake god. No corroborating evidence had ever been found that indicated that Seti ever really existed, and yet the myth persisted, references found in papyri scattered throughout the region. It was said that, cursed and entombed in his sarcophagus as punishment for his transgressions, Seti would walk the earth again after five thousand years, doomed to an eternity of wandering.

But gleaming in the lantern light of the dig was what the team was certain was the final resting place of Seti. The facts were irrefutable. The figure sculpted onto the sarcophagus wore a torc that not only signified the mummy within to have been a king, but the style of the torc dated the sarcophagus to a time before the Sphinx had been built. The hieroglyphics proclaimed him to be Seti, the one who had defied the god Setekh, just as the legend had claimed, and spoke of the curse in great detail.

Most interestingly, the sarcophagus had proven impossible to open. Crowbars snapped when applied under the lid. Chisels, no matter how hard they were hammered, could not move the lid a hairsbreadth. True to the myth of Seti, no man could open the tomb until the curse was lifted.

Could the rest be true as well? Would Seti awake in

just another half century, fully restored after five thousand years? He would if Ethan's translations of the hieroglyphics and his dating of the tomb, were accurate.

It was a bet that the small group of anthropologists was willing to take. For fifty years they'd kept their discovery a secret from the rest of the world. Perry used his position as a curator with the National Museum of Natural History in New York to secret the sarcophagus away. It had remained hidden in the basement of the Museum for a half a century, untouched and unviewed by anyone but himself.

Three of the team, Petrovski, Roman, and Hill, had left Egypt to pursue careers in academia, all three becoming full professors at prestigious universities. They'd lived comfortable lives, retiring within ten years of each other. Now all three lived in retirement communities in Florida, golfing and basking in the warm sun, waiting for their chance at immortality.

Ethan – the least scrupulous of all of them, had transformed himself from an anthropologist into a grave robber. He'd pillaged site after site, stealing Egyptian artifacts and selling them on the black market. Over the years, he'd parlayed his wealth into a fortune.

All the while Perry had continued to slave away in the bowels of the Museum, as poor as a church mouse, the ever faithful watchdog.

He hadn't cared. When Seti awoke and they had drained the secret of immortality from his veins, wealth would mean little. Perry would be a god.

Now the one slim straw Perry had been grasping at was gone, and all because of Ethan's egotistical claim that his data had been foolproof.

Perry ground his teeth as impotent rage washed over him in great waves. Damn Logan Ashton! If he hadn't been forced by Administration to take Logan on as an assistant, then Seti would have awoken to find Perry waiting for him, not that snot-nosed graduate student. Perhaps Perry might have been able to garner the secret of everlasting life from Seti before Ethan and the others were even aware that Seti had returned! Perry would have had the entire world at his feet and Ethan's wealth in his pocket.

Now he'd be lucky if he survived long enough to see Seti recaptured, to witness what the miracle of his rejuvenation had wrought. Perry's health was on a serious decline. His heart had been irreparably damaged by the treatment for his liver disease. The doctors had given him a month or so to live.

Pain clawed at Perry's chest as his anger grew. He removed a prescription bottle from his coat pocket, emptying a small white tablet onto his palm. Placing it under his tongue, he forced himself to relax and let the nitroglycerin work.

Perry slid the bottom drawer of his desk open, taking out a legal pad and an envelope.

It was only a matter of time before Seti would be found, and Logan with him. Unfortunately, Perry now realized that Ethan only needed Seti, and no one else.

Not even Perry.

He'd been a fool to believe that Ethan would allow him to share in whatever miracle Seti's blood had to offer. If his physical ailments didn't kill him, he could be certain that Ethan would.

Removing his pen from his breast pocket, Dr. Lincoln Perry began the last letter he would ever write.

Ethan hung up the phone, swiveling in his chair to look out of the window of his penthouse office at the city that sprawled at his feet.

He'd spent years trafficking on the black market at great personal peril, using his gains to set up bank accounts in Switzerland, offshore in the Bahamas, and a few fat ones right here in the States under dummy corporations. His plan was much simpler than his convoluted bank accounts. As soon as Seti was revived, he was going to drain him of every last ounce of his blood, dissect him under a microscope, and do anything and everything in his considerable power to isolate whatever it was that made Seti immortal. And then Ethan was going to use his findings to cheat death forever.

Of course, the other four members of his group thought the same thing, but Ethan knew that they could never be trusted to keep secret their findings. He planned on killing them all once they were no longer needed.

As a matter of fact, with only a month to go until D-Day, he'd already sent a couple of men down to Florida to see that Petrovski, Roman, and Hill didn't live long enough to collect their next social security checks.

He'd thought to allow Perry to live a while longer. Ethan needed him to keep watch over Seti's sarcophagus, but had decided that the moment the lid cracked open, Perry would be as dead as any of the fossils in the Museum.

Now, all of Ethan's carefully laid plans were at risk because of some idiotic, meddling graduate student who'd managed somehow to wake Seti and had spirited him away from the Museum.

Damn it! Well, one thing was for certain. He didn't need Perry anymore.

He picked up the phone and placed two brief calls. One to a man who owed Ethan a favor or two - a man with tissue-thin morals and a very big gun.

The other call was to a private detective agency that

Ethan had dealt with on numerous occasions. Discreet and trustworthy, willing to bend the law when necessary, he put them on the trail of Logan Ashton and his new friend, Seti.

CHAPTER SEVEN

If you're selling Girl Scout cookies or want to recruit me for the neighborhood watch program, be warned that I have a very short temper and a very big Louisville Slugger."

"Jason! It's Logan! Buzz us in!" Logan said, when Jason's sleepy, irritated voice sounded on the apartment building's intercom.

"Since when is there more than one of you?"

"Just press the freakin' buzzer, Jase!" Logan said, even as memories of their first meeting replayed themselves in his head and heart.

Jason had been Logan's college roommate, and the first to suspect Logan's proclivities. At the time Logan had been out to himself but to no one else. Jason helped him feel comfortable in his own skin, shown him that Logan needed no one's approval.

He remembered what happened moments after outing himself to Jason. One minute Logan had been laying on his bed trying futilely to memorize the human reproductive system, worrying about how his confession was going to change his relationship with his roommate, and the next he'd been flat on his back receiving his first ever blow job from a man. He returned the favor, hesitantly, unsure of himself, but quickly growing more confident. From that day on Logan was firmly, unabashedly out.

Jason was his best friend, as close as any brother could be, and it only seemed natural that he was the one Logan turned to when he found himself needing a safe haven.

But even so, Jason could be a little annoying. Like now.

As soon as he heard the grating, buzzing sound, Logan pushed open the dark green front door of Jason's apartment building. Having seen its last best day sometime in the late sixties, the building was in sore need of more than a simple facelift. It needed a complete body overhaul, as evidenced by the cracked and water-spotted walls and the sagging bellies that decorated the ceiling of the stairwell.

Dim yellow lights flickered, casting the stairs with ochre shadows as Logan led Seti up the five flights to Jason's apartment. There was an elevator in the building, but Logan didn't trust it enough to ever use it. It wasn't much more than a glorified dumb waiter, creaking and groaning as it jerked itself up and down the elevator shaft. In Logan's opinion, it was much safer to take the stairs and chance a heart attack than risk plummeting to his death in that sardine can that masqueraded as an elevator.

Apartment 509 was halfway down the hall on the left. Logan pounded on the door, impatient to get himself and Seti inside and out of sight. "Jason! C'mon, open up!" he yelled, banging so hard that he rattled the door on its hinges.

"Patience is not your personal virtue, is it?" Jason grumbled when Logan pushed past him the instant he unlocked the door, dragging Seti in along after him. "Who's he?"

"A friend. Look, Jase, I'm in trouble."

"He got you pregnant? You slut."

"Will you just shut up and listen?" Logan snarled as Jason chuckled and locked the door. "This is serious."

"Okay, okay," Jason said, putting up both hands as if afraid Logan was going to take a swing at him. Truthfully, Logan was so wound up at the moment that it wasn't outside the realm of possibility. "What's wrong?"

"I...well, it's a long story," Logan replied. "Suffice it to say that I no longer work at the Museum. As a matter of fact, I'm sort of on the run."

"Logan, what did you do?" Jason asked, his voice growing quiet. His eyes shifted from Logan to Seti and back again. "It has to do with him, doesn't it?" It was more of a statement than a question.

"Yeah, it does. This is Seti, and he's...well, he's a lot older than he looks."

"What's his age got to do with anything? C'mon, Logan. You're starting to scare me. Spill."

"Okay, but you won't believe me. The truth is that he's a five thousand year old mummy, and I'm in trouble for stealing him from the Museum."

Jason snorted, rolling his eyes. "Ri-ight. Okay, I don't know what fossilized shit you've been smoking down in the Dungeon, but I want some, and shame on you for not sharing."

"Jason, I'm serious. I'm not high. I-"

"Must you defend yourself to this gnat?" Seti asked, standing tall next to Logan, scowling down at Jason. "He is annoying." Logan didn't know if he wanted to agree with Seti, or kick him in the shins for being so damned arrogant.

"Jason is the one with a place for us to hide, Seti. You need to get off your high horse and be grateful that he even let us in the door," Logan admonished. He put his hand on Jason's shoulder. "I'm sorry, bud. Really. He's a little rough around the edges."

"Rough? His edges could cut diamonds," Jason frowned, looking up at Seti. "Listen, big guy, I've been friends with Logan since-"

"Friends. Do you mean that you are lovers?" Seti asked, his scowl deepening until his sleek black brows met, his eyes narrowing. Logan could almost hear Seti's muscles clenching. Although why Seti was suddenly fixated on Logan's love life was beyond him. He probably thought of Logan as his slave and was having proprietary issues.

"No, we aren't," Logan answered for Jason. "Seti, what's wrong with you? We're just friends, and anyway, that's none of your damn business!"

"Why do you want to know?" Jason countered. "Are you two-"

"No!" Logan repeated, feeling his cheeks blush furiously. The sooner he steered the conversation away from that particular subject, the better off he'd be. He turned to Jason. "Where are Chris and Leo?"

"Interviews. So who is he, really?" Jason asked, still frowning at Seti, who glared back, bristling.

"I am Seti, King of the Children of Set," Seti answered pompously. "What of this Chris and Leo? Are they your lovers?"

"No, Seti, we're not now and we never were anything more than friends! Will you please concentrate on the real problem?" Logan growled. "Us. Fugitives. Remember?"

"The Children of Set? What's that? A cult?" Jason asked. He and Seti were eyeing each other like two dogs about to fight over a bone, making Logan exceedingly uncomfortable.

"Look, could we all please sit down?" Logan asked, desperate to get some space between Jason and Seti before one of them attacked the other. He knew without a doubt, after having witnessed the maelstrom in the bar, which the victor would be and he didn't want to see Jason hurt. Not only was Seti twice Jason's size, he had powers that Logan couldn't explain. "I've had a really shitty day and I need a good, stiff drink."

"You? Drink something more powerful than a draft beer? Shit, you really must be in trouble!" Jason said. He suddenly looked worried, as if he hadn't believed a word Logan had said up until that moment. "Come on. I'll break out a bottle and you can fill me in."

Seti only grunted, but followed closely behind Logan as Jason led them to the kitchen table. Logan slid gratefully into one of the chairs, Seti taking the one to his immediate right. He looked out of place, as if he belonged on a throne instead of a spindly chair bought at Wal-Mart.

Jason opened the freezer, removing a bottle of vodka, and returned to the table with it. He placed three glasses in front of him, cracking open the bottle.

Pouring them each a stiff one, he slid a Flintstones Grape Jelly jar in front of Seti. Logan rolled his eyes, glad that the prehistoric reference was lost on Seti.

"L'chaim," Jason said, lifting his glass.

To life. How appropriate, Logan thought, tossing the shot back. He noticed Seti sniff the liquid, his lip curling in distaste. "If you don't want yours, I'll take it," Logan said, reaching for the jelly jar.

Seti snatched it out of his reach, frowning at Logan. Tilting the glass to his lips, he drank it down. The look on his face was priceless as the alcohol burned a trail to his stomach.

Sheesh. He looked ready to snap my fingers off if I touched his glass, Logan thought. Then again, he silently admonished himself, if I'd gone five millennia without a drink, I'd be a little testy, too.

"So, tell me, Logan. What gives? What's this guy got to do with you being in trouble?" Jason asked, pouring them all another round.

"I told you the truth, Jason. He's a mummy who was under a curse-"

"Jesus, Logan! What did I do to make you think that you can't trust me with the truth?" Jason snapped, slamming the bottle down on the table.

Seti shot up from his chair, his eyes hard, glaring at Jason. Logan grabbed his arm, pulling on it. "Sit down, Seti. He's got a right to be upset. It does sound preposterous, you know. All of this." Relief flooded him as Seti sat again, if reluctantly. Honestly, the man had a hair trigger temper.

Logan realized that Jason was never going to believe him. Hell, Logan wouldn't believe Logan either, if he hadn't seen the sarcophagus and Seti's little storm trick in the bar with his own two eyes.

"Seti," Logan said, sighing, "Can you give Jason a small demonstration? Nothing major, like the one in the bar. Just enough to show him what you can do."

Seti looked annoyed. "Why must I prove anything to him? He claims to be your friend, and yet doubts your word."

"Please, Seti?" Damn it, Logan hated having to beg, but it was crucial that Jason believed them, or Jason could find himself in trouble for harboring a pair of fugitives. He wanted to be certain that Jason knew exactly what he was getting himself into by helping them.

Seti huffed, but looked over into the living room. There, sitting next to the sofa was a large fish tank in which a pair of pale blue angelfish swam. Seti pointed a finger at it, his lips moving silently.

Suddenly, the water in the fish tank began to bubble, then swirl, rising out of the fish tank in a twisting waterspout. The fish, along with a plastic castle and a few fake corals spun dizzyingly in the watery funnel as it rose a full five feet into the air above the tank.

With a splash, the funnel collapsed back into the tank, water sloshing over the sides onto the floor. The fish teetered in the water before slowly beginning to swim again.

"Holy shit!" Jason cried, jumping up. He raced into the living room, examining the tank from all angles. "How the fuck did you do that?"

"That's what I've been trying to tell you, Jason. He's an Egyptian king - and evidently a sorcerer - who was cursed and mummified five thousand years ago. His sentence was up as of today, and he's rejuvenated," Logan said tiredly. He looked up at Seti. "Thanks, Seti. That was perfect."

Seti grunted, but there was a strained look in his eyes.

"Did that hurt you, Seti?" Logan asked, suddenly concerned. He hadn't thought whether or not it was painful for Seti to use his magic.

"No. I am just weak," Seti replied. "It will pass."

"Okay. Okay," Jason mumbled, coming back into the kitchen and taking his seat. He watched Seti with wide eyes, as if he was awestruck and waiting for Seti's next impressive trick. "That was fucking awesome! Have you thought about doing Vegas?"

"Yeah, he's the next David Copperfield," Logan said dryly, refilling his glass for the third time. The vodka was going down smoother now, and his head was starting to buzz pleasantly. "Our problem, in case you were wondering, is that Perry knew about Seti. He had him squirreled away in a locked room."

"Why? What good would that do the Museum?" Jason asked. "If he's authentic- "

"He is. He's the real deal, Jason," Logan repeated tiredly.

"If he is authentic," Jason continued stubbornly, "then

why not have him on display?"

"I don't think the Museum knew about Seti. His sarcophagus looked as if it was made of pure gold. I figure Perry was counting on selling it on the black market when he retires at the end of the year. Since I was the last one in the Dungeon, Perry must think I broke into the sarcophagus and stole the mummy. He's already sent a couple of security guards out after us." Logan cast a sideways look at Seti. "We had a little trouble at The Bones."

"Shit! That sucks, Logan. You didn't do anything wrong! Goddamn Perry. The good news is if he was really hiding that sarcophagus without the Museum's knowledge, then he'll never be able to go to the police with it. Look, you both need to stay here for a while, until things cool off," Jason said, smiling. "Seti here can entertain us with his prestidigitation and feats extraordinaire."

"Thanks, Jase," Logan replied, downing another shot. "I knew I could count on you. It'll just be until I can figure out what to do." His eyelids felt heavy and his head and the room were spinning pleasantly. "I think I need to lay down now."

"No prob. Take my room. I'll bunk in with Leo," Jason said.

Logan tried to stand up, but his knees didn't want to cooperate. He teetered then fell back into his chair.

"Jesus, Logan. You need to drink more. You're such a fucking lightweight!" Jason laughed. "Come on. I'll help you- "

"I will help him," Seti growled. He stood and picked Logan up bodily, scooping the man easily into his arms, cradling Logan like an infant. "Where is the room in which we may rest?"

If Logan hadn't been three-sheets to the wind, he might have had the presence of mind to inform Seti that they would not be resting anywhere. He would take Jason's room and Seti would take the couch. But as it was, he could barely keep his eyes open. His head lolled against Seti's bicep.

Jason pointed the way to the bedroom, and Logan's head bounced against the hard muscle of Seti's arm as he was carried through the living room. Once inside the bedroom, he found himself staring at the ceiling as Seti laid him down carefully on the bed.

He heard the door lock and felt someone tugging at his clothing. A thick comforter was pulled up over him, and he snuggled happily into its warmth.

The last thing he remembered was a weight dipping the mattress at his side before his eyes rolled back in his head and Logan passed out.

CHAPTER EIGHT

Logan dreamed that he was making love.

Strong hands that knew their way around a man's body slid over his flesh, leaving trails of tingling warmth in their wake.

Soft lips and a hot, wet tongue tortured his nipples, flicking and pulling at the peaked buds, shooting bolts of pleasure into his groin. Logan's nipples had always been sensitive, and his dream lover took full advantage of that fact, working them unmercifully until Logan moaned and writhed, whimpering piteously.

His cock was hard, needy, his balls swollen and aching. Logan's entire body thrummed with want, his fingers twisting in the sheets as every inch of him screamed for release. His every nerve ending sizzled, taunted and tormented by a tongue and hands that knew exactly where to touch, where to taste to drive Logan wild.

Logan's entire body was exquisitely hypersensitive, feeling every touch, no matter how slight: fingers brushing through his pubic hair, skimming teasingly over the flesh of his erection; a rigid, red hot shaft pressing against Logan's hip, digging into his flesh as if trying to make its way inside his body; lips nibbling at the pebbled flesh of his nipple. He craved to touch his lover, taste him, devour him, but he was trapped between the mattress and a pair of relentless lips and talented hands. Instead, he mewled with frustration, wriggling under a lover who was relentlessly burying him under waves of pleasure.

He subconsciously fought against waking. This dream was so real. His dreams had always been ambiguous until now; gauzy sequences flitting one to another that would unerringly leave him awake and alone in his bed with an aching hard-on, unfulfilled. None had ever been like this. Nothing had ever come close to this. He could feel the heat and the trail of wetness that his lover's cock left against his thigh, could hear his soft groans of pleasure, could smell his strong, musky scent.

No matter how much Logan wished to remain tethered to his dream, he began to awaken. The cobwebs of sleep slowly cleared, but the sensations of being touched and licked did not.

His eyes flew open as he realized that he wasn't alone in his bed, and that he hadn't really been dreaming.

Logan gasped as he looked down at the dark head that lapped at his nipple. "Seti? What are you doing?" he cried, tearing himself away from Seti's warm mouth and teasing fingers. He scooted up until his back pressed against the headboard, staring with wide eyes at Seti, who slowly lifted his head and met his gaze.

Seti's pupils were dilated with lust, making his dark brown eyes look black. As Logan watched, the pink tip of his tongue lazily peeked out between Seti's full lips, wetting them. "I am in need, Logan," he said, his voice deep and rough.

"You...we...don't..." For the life of him, Logan couldn't form a coherent argument. He swallowed hard, realizing that his body was rebelling against him, ignoring the list of reasons that his mind was forming of why this was a very bad idea. His body wanted Seti. Needed him. Would have him, regardless of whatever reservations Logan's mind might have. "Seti," he said again, this time whispering his name almost like a prayer.

Seti smiled at Logan, lifting himself up on one elbow. His dark gaze held Logan spellbound, unable to move, scarcely able to breathe. Seti's head moved closer, until his lips smashed against Logan's in a scorching kiss that curled Logan's toes and hardened his cock painfully.

He tasted of vodka and something else, something primal, as if Seti was made of the earth itself instead of flesh and blood. "Open for me," he commanded, and Logan instantly obeyed, parting his lips to accept Seti's tongue.

Warm, soft, and wet, it invaded Logan's mouth like a conquering army, sweeping it, testing and tasting until Logan moaned and began to kiss Seti in return.

Hungry. Logan was starving, ravenous for more of Seti's taste. Greedily, he sucked on Seti's lower lip, pulling the plump bit of flesh into his mouth. He wanted this man. Wanted to slide his body against Seti's, feel every inch of Seti's satiny flesh against his own. Wanted Seti inside of him, filling him up until he was ready to burst. Wanted. Needed. Now.

Logan groaned, his hands sliding over Seti's flesh, trying to map it, to commit every inch to his memory. His fingers closed over the thickness of Seti's cock, its sweet heat burning his palm. "Touch me, Seti," he begged. He would have been shocked to hear the pleading in his voice, but he was too overwhelmed by the feel, taste, and smell of Seti to comprehend, or care, how needy he sounded. He wanted Seti, all of him, in every conceivable way.

Seti's moan was music to Logan's ears. His lips laid a trail of love bites along the tender flesh of Logan's throat, his tongue soothing the small hurts. His hand wrapped around Logan's cock, squeezing it gently until Logan knew beyond a shadow of a doubt that he was going to come.

There was no holding back. He felt his release boiling up, ready to rocket through his system like a runaway freight train, unstoppable. "Seti... " Logan groaned, rocking his hips up into Seti's fist.

"Ah, yes..." Seti's voice was palpable, caressing Logan's ears just as his hands stroked Logan's flesh. "Give yourself to me, Logan. Mine. Say you are mine."

"Yours..." Logan grunted through clenched teeth as flames Seti had kindled within him exploded into a firestorm, sweeping through him at light speed. He cried out, his back arching, every muscle in his body seizing and contracting, growing as rigid as his cock had been. Pinpoint stars danced behind his eyelids, his breath catching in his chest as he rode wave after wave of ecstasy.

Floating back down into himself, Logan opened his eyes, looking at Seti from under heavy lids. "Mmm," he murmured, not quite able to speak. He felt completed, sated, boneless, warm and lazy.

Smiling, Seti's eyes twinkled mischievously as he traced a finger through the thick laces of semen that coated Logan's chest and belly. Lifting his finger to his mouth, Seti licked it clean. Logan's cock twitched, watching Seti's tongue curl with a pearly drop of come on its pink tip before disappearing into his mouth. "Mine," Seti said again, firmly this time. Logan could hear the possessiveness in that deep voice and his body responded to it, his cock stirring again.

Seti's strong hands urged Logan up, onto his knees. He looked over his shoulder at Seti, who was positioning himself behind Logan. A worry briefly teased at Logan's mind. No condom. No lubricant. Then again, he reasoned, Seti hadn't had sex with anyone for five thousand years. Chances were good that he was clean. As for the lubricant...

Spitting into his hand, Seti slicked himself. Nature's

Best, Logan thought wildly as Seti pressed the head of his thick erection against Logan's asshole. He felt the burn as Seti began to push himself into Logan's body.

Logan was no virgin. True, he hadn't taken a long-term lover, but he wasn't a stranger to sex, either. But he felt himself stretched as if he was, his body protesting the thickness of the cock that invaded it. Goddamn! Logan knew that Seti was big, had admired his cock when Logan has first seen it after Seti had awoken. But now it felt as if Seti's erection was enormous, as if it was a phallic stone fetish, freakishly large. As if it would split Logan wide open, into two neat halves.

"Relax your body, Logan. Let me in." Seti's hands rubbed his lower back soothingly then smoothed slowly over the cheeks of his ass, cupping them, separating them.

Logan bit his lip, consciously trying to obey Seti's order. Slowly, he felt the tension he'd been feeling leave him, felt Seti slip deeper into his body until Logan was filled completely.

He gasped as he felt an instant connection with Seti that went far deeper than his cock. It sparked within Logan's core, his veins carrying it along with his blood throughout his body until Logan was utterly suffused with the feeling. It was as if he and Seti were no longer two distinct entities, but one, hearts beating in sync.

"Mine," Seti moaned, beginning to move within Logan's body. Slowly, his cock withdrew and returned. Each time it left him, Logan was filled with remorse, with an emptiness that was difficult to bear. Each time it returned to refill Logan's body, it renewed Logan's sense of connection with Seti, permeating him with an elation that he'd never known before, a sense of belonging that he'd never tasted.

Over and over the cycle repeated itself, Seti's rhythm

growing faster, his thrusts harder, until Seti's roar rang in Logan's ears and his seed filled Logan's body to overflowing. Sweet pressure filled Logan's channel with liquid heat and his cock with blood, another orgasm ripping unexpectedly through him, wringing a cry from his lips. Untouched, his cock painted the sheets with his seed, tangible proof of their lovemaking.

Logan collapsed as Seti's weight pushed him down over the cooling, sticky mess. He felt weightless, completely and utterly satisfied. He sighed then noticed how difficult it was to draw in another breath with Seti laying on top of him.

"Seti. Can't. Breathe," he gasped, trying to wiggle out from under Seti's heavy weight. The man must weigh well over two hundred pounds, Logan realized, and all of it muscle.

He felt rather than heard Seti's chuckle rumble in his chest as Seti rolled off of him. One arm remained across Logan's shoulders, a hand soothing over the tired and totally relaxed muscles of his back. "You are mine now, Logan."

"Yeah, you said that. A few times, as a matter of fact. Exactly what do you mean by 'mine,' anyway? I'm not your slave, Seti, if that's what you're thinking."

"No, of course not. I would not have claimed you had you been a slave. Slaves are for temporary pleasure, not bonding."

"Bonding?" Logan repeated, the definition of the word dancing through his mind. It sounded permanent. Like something you'd need super glue to achieve.

"Yes. You are mine. I have claimed you, and you have acquiesced. We are lovers now. We are bonded."

"Oh," Logan breathed. He felt his cheeks heat, his belly warming with a sweet, tingly feeling. "You really want me? I mean, for more than just tonight?"

"Yes." Seti's answer was simple, but filled Logan with conflicting emotions, chief among them a giddy happiness that Seti wanted him, and a razor-sharp fear of being hurt by the man.

"You say that now, but you've only been awake for less than a day, Seti. Wait until you see the guys running around this city. All hard bodies and six packs, perfect faces, perfect tans...and they're all going to be tripping over themselves to get to you. You might want to hold off with this bonding business until after you see what you could have. I'm nothing compared to them."

"Who has filled your head with such nonsense?" Seti growled, his hand cupping Logan's chin. His gaze pierced Logan, searing him to the bone. "There can be no one but you for me. I knew the instant that I saw you that I would have you, that you were born to be mine. I saw it in your eyes."

"My eyes?"

Seti's gaze softened, his lips tilting in a sad smile. "Yes. I knew someone once with your eyes. I can see a similar soul looking out at me through yours. He was much like you, gentle and sweet. I lost him. I will not lose you."

"I'm not anybody but myself," Logan whispered. "You can't expect me to be."

"I do not wish you to be anyone other than yourself. But know that I will not let you go, will not give you up. I would lay down my life to protect you, Logan. I failed to do that for Ashai, but I will not do so again."

"I don't believe in reincarnation, Seti."

"I did not say that you were Ashai reincarnated. I said you shared the same gentle soul. That is enough."

CHAPTER NINE

The following morning found Logan and Seti sitting at the kitchen table covered in half-empty cereal boxes, bowls, a carton of orange juice and coffee cups. Logan had eaten breakfast while trying to answer a barrage of questions from Chris and Leo, who'd arrived at the apartment with the sun, and explaining to Seti why meat was not always a staple at every meal.

Eventually, the discussion was moved into the living room. Sitting on the couch, they went through a repeat of the day before, trying to convince Chris and Leo of who and what Seti was, including an encore of Seti's Great Fish Tank Tornado trick.

By the time they'd peeled Chris and Leo off the ceiling, both had been converted into true believers.

"How lucky can one guy get, Logan? You get all the breaks! First, you land an Assistant's position, get put on the fast track to becoming Curator, and then you get a hunk like him to cuddle up to at night. It's not fair!" Leo whined.

"Oh, yeah. I'm a lucky bastard all right. In case you didn't pick up on it the first time around, I'm a wanted man. Chances are good that I've lost my position at the Museum and the only way I'll see a Curator's office is on the guided tour." Logan said, rolling his eyes. He felt he was lucky, up to a point, even if he wouldn't admit it. After all, he did have some kind of a relationship blossoming with Seti – although what kind of relationship and how stable it would be was still up in the air. There was something uncomfortable about Seti's assertion that Logan reminded him of his former lover, and that made Logan a little leery of any commitment.

Then again, Seti was six feet-something of pure sex, with the face of a movie star and the body of a Greek god, and who made Logan feel things he'd only read about in books. For the time being, Logan was perfectly content to suffer along in silence.

That is, if he didn't find himself locked up in a jail cell with a cellmate named Butch and a broomstick handle shoved up his ass.

Chris and Leo, once their shock at Seti's fish tank trick had worn off, spent the next fifteen minutes trying to figure out how Seti had performed his little bit of fishy magic without the benefit of strings, mirrors, or hallucinogenic drugs. Leave it to the nerds to try to apply practical science to something that was clearly supernatural in origin.

"I feel compelled to ask, since no one else at this table seems to have half a brain between them," Chris said, "Have you thought of going to the police, Logan?"

"The police. Right. Exactly what should I tell them, Chris? Oh, yes, officers, I was there when the sarcophagus was destroyed, but I didn't do it. He did it. The mummy," Logan said sarcastically, nodding toward Seti. "Yeah, that'll buy me a Prozac cocktail and a one way ticket to Cell Block B."

"I see your point," Chris answered. "Basically, you're screwed, and not in the good way."

"Yeah," Logan said, thinking that he had been screwed

the good way, the incredibly, unbelievably good way, but the others didn't need to hear that tidbit of information. "I just wish I had a way to find out if Perry was really hiding that sarcophagus from the Museum. If so, then maybe I could get him to call off his dogs."

"You could go and talk to him," Leo said, flopping down on the sofa next to Seti.

Logan frowned, noticing Leo rubbing his thigh against Seti's leg. Funny how one mind-blowing session of sexual aerobics could make a guy feel proprietary. He felt unaccountably relieved when Seti tossed Leo an annoyed look and slid closer to Logan.

"That might not be a bad idea, Logan. I'm sure Seti here could do some razzle dazzle to convince him of who he is, which would let you off the hook, whether Perry was hiding it or not," Jason said as Chris nodded in agreement.

"Maybe. But I'd be taking a helluva chance. What if he wasn't hiding the sarcophagus? What if the police are already involved?" Logan asked. "I'd be arrested."

"I will not allow anyone to take you from me," Seti said. "They would die before I allowed them to touch you."

"Seti, you can't go around killing people."

"I can if they threaten you."

"No, you can't."

"You are mistaken. I can. It would be easy."

"That's not what I meant. I know you can – I've seen what you can do. I meant that you shouldn't. I don't want to be responsible for anyone getting hurt, Seti. Promise me that you won't hurt anyone."

"Logan…"

"Promise me!"

"Ashai said these same words to me before, Logan, in another life, another time. I gave him my word then and because I did not act, he was lost to me. I will not allow that to happen again!" Seti roared, jumping to his feet.

Logan looked up at Seti with wide eyes. Seti was beautiful in his fury. He towered over the sofa, more than six feet of bristling muscle, his handsome face drawn into an intense scowl, eyes narrowed and nostrils flaring.

This was what it felt like to have someone who wanted you, wanted to protect you at all costs, to move heaven and earth and destroy both if necessary to keep you at his side. How much must he have loved the man called Ashai, his lover in ancient Egypt? Logan bit his lip, feeling his emotions bubble up, tightening his chest and burning at the corners of his eyes. Some of it was jealousy toward a man long dead; more than anything, he wished those feelings were for him, and not for a memory of someone that Seti still carried in his heart.

"What's he mean, 'in another life,' Logan?" Chris asked, frowning at Logan. "Who's Ashai?"

"Never mind that, Chris. That's between Seti and me," Logan said. "Sit down, Seti. Please? I'm not going anywhere."

Seti sat, but Logan could still feel his tension. He fairly crackled with it, his muscles bunching, drawing him up as tight as a tiger readying to pounce.

"Look, you and Seti don't have to go anywhere. We can go," Jason said, indicating himself, Leo, and Chris. "First, we can Google a search on the net, check out the newspaper sites. If Perry is on the level, he'll have reported the break-in and something that bizarre will surely make it into the dailies. If not, then we can go to the Museum, ask a few questions. See if there's any buzz about the sarcophagus and Logan."

"That's a great idea!" Leo smiled. "You know the graduate student crowd, Logan. They're the best source for gossip. They know everything that goes on in the Museum."

"I don't know. I don't want to put you in danger, or get you involved in any of this, guys," Logan said, shaking his head.

"Good! It's decided then," Jason grinned.

Logan had to smile. Jason had an annoying habit of ignoring Logan and everyone else who disagreed with his ideas. "All right. But promise me that you'll be discreet, and more than that, that you'll be careful."

"Yes, Mommy," Jason said, laughing.

"It's not funny, Jason. I'm serious."

"I know, I know. We'll be fine," Jason said. "Come on, let's go."

Logan began to pace before his friends had even left the apartment. He moved from one end of the living room to the other and back again like a pendulum, his hands shoved deeply into his pockets, his chin tucked down.

Seti could feel his tension and understood it, as well as Logan's reaction to it. He'd had occasion to feel the same anxiety once upon a time. Sending out scouts to seek information from the enemy's camp was always risky. But while Seti's concern at the time had been for the ramifications for his camp, should his enemies discover the spies he'd sent, he understood that Logan's distress was caused by fear for his friends' safety.

Ashai had been much the same.

Beautiful in a way most men could never dream of being, Ashai had possessed a soul that mirrored his physical being. He had been sweet and tender, patient beyond measure, and wise beyond his years. Ashai had faced Seti at his worst and gentled him with a single look or touch. His loss had decimated Seti, had pained him more than any wound Seti had ever sustained in battle.

Seti braced himself for the onslaught of rage and the burn of tears that always filled him when his thoughts turned to Ashai. For ages Seti had seethed silently in his tomb, unable to scream or cry, tortured by the memories of him.

Surprisingly, instead of the expected wave of fury there came only fond remembrance. The suffocating sadness that had always before overwhelmed Seti had been tempered with wistfulness, and the pain was no longer raw and devastating.

And Seti knew why.

In his heart of hearts, Seti believed that he had not only been released from his curse, but had been given another chance. He believed he had been given an opportunity to redeem himself, to prove that he was a better man and had learned from his mistakes.

He had been given Ashai again.

Not in the same physical shell. Logan was of a slighter build than Ashai had been, his coloring was much lighter, his facial features different. But those dazzling green eyes were unmistakable, as was the ka that looked back at Seti through them.

Logan Ashton had been born a man of the twenty-first century, but his soul was five thousand years old. Seti's eyes had recognized him the moment he'd first seen Logan standing wide-eyed in the Museum, and his body had confirmed it when they'd made love the night before. No other man aside from Ashai had ever made Seti feel so complete, so fully and wholly satisfied, or so connected with another human being.

Five thousand years ago, Seti had made the unforgivable error of allowing himself to be seduced by power and greed. He had not been diligent in his oath; he'd let Ashai be taken from under his nose and had not acted swiftly enough to save his lover.

Seti would not, upon his life, make that same mistake again.

But at the moment Logan did not need to be protected. He needed succor, distraction from his worries, and ease of the tension that knotted his shoulders and knit his smooth brow. On the eve of battle in his old life, Ashai would have seen to Seti's needs, easing the stress that tightened his muscles. Today, Seti could give Logan that same care, although it would take from Seti something he had never before offered to give anyone, including Ashai.

Not once, since he was a child playing with colorful stones at his father's feet, had Seti lowered himself to kneel before anyone.

And yet for Logan, he didn't need to think twice. Seti placed himself in Logan's path and dropped gracefully to his knees. Looking up into Logan's questioning eyes, he smiled and reached for the zipper of Logan's jeans.

"Seti! What are you doing-"

"Let me do this for you, Logan. Let me ease your mind," Seti said softly, when Logan pushed his hands away.

"No! Seti, I can't. I'm too worried," Logan said. "Come on. Stand up."

"I kneel before you, Logan. I have never prostrated myself before anyone else. I do this because you need me," Seti confessed. He felt himself blush, something he couldn't ever recall doing before. Still, he couldn't, wouldn't let Logan suffer. He watched as Logan lowered himself to the floor, facing him.

"Seti," Logan said, placing his hands on Seti's cheeks. "I appreciate the thought. Really, I do. And I think I understand how difficult it is for you to make the offer. But the last thing I need right now is a blowjob. If you really want to know what I need, it's just to be held for a while."

Seti nodded, not quite understanding, but willing to give Logan what he asked for. Pulling Logan into his arms, he quietly held the man, both still kneeling on the floor.

After a while, Logan began to squirm. "My knees are killing me, big guy. Can we at least sit on the couch?"

Seti chuckled, nodding. They moved to the sofa. Seti put an arm around Logan's shoulder, and Logan rested his head against Seti's chest. Together, they watched the clock and waited to hear from Logan's friends.

Across the street, in an empty apartment facing Jason's building, a man sat in a lawn chair. He trained a pair of powerful binoculars out of the window, watching the inhabitants of apartment 509.

"Oh, man. Tell me I don't have to watch this again."

"What's going on in there, Joe?" A second man, Harry, sat nearby, working over the remains of a Philly cheese steak sandwich. A long, twisted string of mozzarella cheese dangled from his bottom lip and there was a smear of ketchup on his cheek.

"I think the big one, that Seti guy, is about to go down on the other one. He's trying to unzip Ashton's pants."

"Shit. Again? That's fucking gross," Harry said, wiping his mouth on his sleeve and belching. "Goddamn faggots. Can't keep it in their pants for more than five minutes."

"Oh, wait. No, they moved to the couch. They're just sitting there now. Man, I thought I was going to have to watch the whole fucking freak show again."

"There's only the two of them in there now. Why don't

we move in? What are we waiting for?"

"The boss said that we gotta wait until we can get Ashton and Seti away from each other. Then we're only to take Seti."

"Why wait?"

"I don't know why. I don't ask questions. I say, 'Yes, sir,' and I do as I'm fucking told. And so do you," Joe said, snagging one of Harry's fries. Popping it into his mouth, he returned to his surveillance of the apartment.

CHAPTER TEN

Jason, Chris, and Leo raced up the stairs from the 79th Street subway station, dodging professionals with briefcases, upper crust housewives with frou-frou poodles, students lugging backpacks, and sightseers snapping cameras, turning onto Central Park West. The museum loomed up before them, a steady stream of tourists threading in and out of the front doors.

Stopping only long enough to purchase tickets, they made their way through the crowds and into the Museum.

"Where should we look first?" Leo asked, craning his head to see over the throng of people that filled the Main Lobby. The boys pushed their way through the crowd, heading toward the exhibits. "The cafeteria?"

"Maybe we should split up," Chris said, as they paused at the entrance to the Hall of Mammals. "We could cover more ground that way."

"No, something tells me that we should stick together," Jason said. "I'm getting some pretty nasty vibes in here. I don't like it."

"Please tell me you're not going to do the Amazing Karnak schtick again," Chris said. "It's really getting old, Jase. When are you going to admit that you don't really have any psychic-"

"He was right about Logan and Seti, Chris. After what we saw Seti do in the apartment, how can you still doubt Jason?" Leo demanded.

That gave Chris pause. "Well, that could have been a lucky guess."

"Yeah, and I could be the Tooth Fairy, but it's highly doubtful."

"Not the 'fairy' part. You've got that down pat," Chris grumbled, earning himself a half-hearted punch in the arm from Leo.

"Let's head down to the labs. We need to find a familiar face who knows what scuttlebutt is going around the Museum," Jason said, ignoring Chris and Leo's banter. He led them toward the stairs, keeping an eye out for security. Seeing no one looking in their direction, he opened the door and the three of them slipped into the stairwell.

One floor below the Main Lobby and one above the Dungeon lay a maze of laboratories where acquisitions were carbon-dated, x-rayed, and put through a battery of other tests to determine authenticity and age. Here was where the boys had their best chance of finding an acquaintance that could fill them in on what Perry had done – or had not done - about the break-in.

Peering into the window of each lab as they passed it, Jason finally spotted a woman who he'd taken several classes with while in school. She was bent over a Bunsen burner, watching a blue liquid bubble in a test tube.

Jason knocked on the door, cracking it open and sticking his head inside the lab. "Hey, Sheila!" he called, smiling when she looked up and returned his grin. "Got a minute?"

"Sure. What are you doing down here, Jason?" she asked, waving them inside the lab. "I didn't know you had a position with the Museum. What department do you work for?"

"I don't," Jason replied. Noting her raised eyebrow, he quickly continued, "I'm here looking for Logan. You remember Logan Ashton, right?"

"Of course. He works for Perry now, doesn't he? He's probably down in the Dungeon."

"Oh, um…yeah. Thanks. We'll head down there next. Oh, hey, did your Department lose anything in the break-in last night? I heard that Perry lost something really valu-able and-"

"Oh, my God! There was a break-in? What did they take?" Sheila exclaimed.

"Didn't Perry mention anything to anyone about it? It's really just a rumor that I've heard." Jason said.

"Oh. You should know better than to listen to rumors, Jason. Did Logan tell you that? He must have been pull-ing your leg. Perry hasn't said a word to anyone about a theft, and you know I would have heard about it if he did. Everyone would have heard about it. Perry is absolutely anal about the Dungeon – he would be screaming bloody murder if someone had broken into his sanctuary."

"Damn that Logan," Jason said, trying to keep the ela-tion out of his voice. "You're right, there must not be anything to it. I should have known better than to trust Logan. He probably just wanted to see how far he could yank my chain. He can be such a dick wad sometimes. Thanks, Sheila."

"No prob."

Outside the lab, Jason looked at Chris and Leo. "Well, my money says that Perry hasn't said a word to anyone about Seti going missing." He jerked his thumb over his shoulder toward the lab. "Sheila was always one of the first ones to know about gossip in school. Stands to rea-son that she'd keep her ear to the ground here, too."

"So, what do we do now?" Leo asked.

"Now? Now we go have ourselves a little chat with Perry," Jason said, turning toward the stairs.

"Whoa, wait a minute," Chris said, grabbing Jason's sleeve. "Are you sure that's such a good idea? What do you plan on asking him? Hey, where'd you put the golden sarcophagus and the missing mummy? You know, the two things no one is supposed to know about?"

"Don't be stupid. We can go down there looking for Logan. See what kind of a reaction we get from Perry when we mention him," Jason replied. "I want to know whether that scumbucket really thinks Logan took the mummy, or if he knows more about Seti than he's letting on."

"You don't think he knows about Seti rejuvenating, do you?" Leo asked.

"I'm telling you, I'm getting really weird vibes about this. I think there's a lot more going on than Perry hoarding an artifact as a nest egg."

"All right, then. After you, O Psychic Wonder," Leo grinned, bowing and gesturing Jason on toward the stairs with a flourish.

Jason shook his head. "You're such a drama queen. Let's go," he said, brushing past Leo.

He led them down the stairs to the level that housed the Dungeon. They threaded their way between the rows of ceiling-to-floor shelves, making their way to the back to Perry's office. The door was closed and the lights off. There was no sign of Perry anywhere.

Leo pointed to the only other door in the room. "That's got to be the room where Perry kept Seti's sarcophagus!" he said. Walking over to the door, he examined it, peering at the smooth wood and bright, shiny metal hinges. "This is new. Perry must have had the old one replaced."

"Is it open?"

Leo grabbed a latex glove from the dispenser on the

wall and snapped it onto his hand. He jiggled the handle, and the door swung open easily. He felt for a switch along the wall and flipped it, turning on the single light fixture. The room was empty.

"He must have gotten rid of it," Chris said. "Why would he get rid of the sarcophagus after keeping it hidden for fifty years?"

"Maybe he didn't want any evidence laying around," Jason finished. "If Perry had said anything to anyone about the break-in, Sheila would have known about it, or at least heard a rumor. But, overnight, Perry had the sarcophagus removed and the door replaced. I'm convinced that Perry had Seti's sarcophagus in here illegally."

"Now what do we do?"

"Now we check Perry's office for evidence."

"Might I remind you that we're not Sam Spade and Company? We're a trio of grad students who don't know their legal asses from their litigious elbows. What you're talking about doing is breaking and entering!" Chris said, frowning.

"It's only a B&E if the door is locked. If it's open, then it's only trespassing," Leo grinned. "Come on. We've come this far. Nobody's home – what can it hurt to take a peek and see what we can find?"

"You go on. I'll keep watch," Chris said, shaking his head. He trotted up the aisle toward the front of the Dungeon.

"You are such a chickenshit," Jason called after him, chuckling. "Okay, here goes." He suddenly paused, his hand hovering over the doorknob to Perry's office. "Something's wrong. Really wrong," he whispered. He felt the blood rush from his head to his feet, leaving him dizzy. While Jason had often gotten "flashes" of feelings before, he'd never felt anything like this. This was more than unsettling. There were vibes coming from Perry's office that were downright terrifying.

"Is it open?" Leo asked.

"I don't know, but...I'm suddenly not sure that I want to see what's inside."

"Then move. I'll do it," Leo said, elbowing Jason out of the way. "And you've got the nerve to call me a drama queen. Sheesh." He turned the knob and pushed open the door to Perry's office. He found and flipped the light switch, instantly flooding the room with light.

Lincoln Perry sat at his desk, head thrown back, his lifeless eyes staring at the ceiling. A single gunshot wound marred the skin on his forehead. Surprisingly, there was very little blood - just a thin trickle down the side of his face and a few spots splattered on the collar of his shirt.

"Holy fucking shit!" Leo gasped, taking a step backwards. "Is he dead?"

"Oh, God. Unless he's into some really fucking weird body modifications, he is," Jason whispered, putting a hand over his mouth, his stomach lurching as his breakfast tried to make a reappearance.

"Guys?" Chris called from the front of the room. "I found something," he said, walking back toward Perry's office. He stopped in his tracks when he saw the looks on Jason and Leo's faces. "Oh, shit. What's happened?"

"It's Perry. He's dead."

"What? Are you sure?" Chris asked, eyes widening.

"About as sure as I can get without performing an autopsy," Leo said, running his hands through his hair. "What are we going to do? We can't just leave him here."

"Maybe he's had a heart attack or something," Chris said, stepping past Leo into Perry's office. "Are you sure he's..." His voice trailed off. "Oh, man. He's been shot!"

"No shit," Jason said. "Any other brilliant observations, Einstein?"

"Did you touch anything?" Chris asked, pinching the bridge of his nose as if he'd suddenly been struck by a terrible headache.

"I had a glove on. I didn't leave any fingerprints," Leo said.

"Okay. Then I say that we get the hell out of here. We can stop at a payphone and call the cops. Tell them where to find Perry and hang up before they can trace the call," Chris said. "Come on. We need to leave. Now."

"What's that?" Jason asked, indicating a white envelope Chris held in his hand.

"I found it in Logan's inbox. I don't know what it is. I haven't opened it," Chris answered as they hurried back toward the stairs.

Forcing themselves to slow down to a walk when they reached the Main Lobby, they made their way out of the Museum. They hit the sidewalk at a run, sped down the block and turned off onto 79th Street, ducking down into the subway.

Chris wrapped his hand in a paper towel snagged from the men's room, while Jason made the call to the police. It was short, sweet, and to the point. "Dr. Lincoln Perry has been murdered. His body in his office at the National Museum of Natural History." He hung up before the 911 Operator could say a word other than "911. What's your emergency?"

None of them breathed a sigh of relief until they were safely seated on the next train leaving the station. It left them six long city blocks from their apartment, but they doubled-timed it all the way back, taking the stairs two at a time and arriving in the living room huffing, puffing, and gasping for air.

"What the hell happened?" Logan asked, jumping up.

"Perry's dead," Jason wheezed, bending over at the waist, trying to get his breath. "He was murdered, Logan."

"Oh my God! Who would want to kill him? Yeah, he was nasty, snooty, and a pain in everyone's ass, but he was harmless," Logan gasped, swaying a little on his feet. "They're going to think I killed him, aren't they?"

Seti put his hands on Logan's shoulders, steadying him.

"No. If it comes down to that, you've got four witnesses who know you've been here at the apartment all night," Chris said. Looking up at Seti, he amended himself. "Well, three witnesses. I don't think Seti can take the stand. I'm pretty sure you need to have been born in this millennia to testify."

"Whoever killed him must have smuggled the sarcophagus out of the Museum, too. It was gone, Logan. And the door had been replaced," Jason said. Walking into the kitchen, he returned with the half-empty bottle of vodka and took a long swallow before passing it to Leo.

"Oh, and I found this in your inbox," Chris said, handing the envelope to Logan.

Logan blinked, as if still in shock. He took the envelope from Chris' hand, his own shaking badly. Sitting down on the couch, he opened it and took out a folded sheet of lined legal paper. "Oh, my God," he said, unfolding it and reading a few of the handwritten lines, "It's from Perry."

CHAPTER ELEVEN

Jason, Chris, and Leo stood close together in a semicircle around Logan, staring down at the letter he held in his hands as if it was a snake that might jump free and bite them. Seti stood slightly apart from them with his arms folded, the look on his face stern.

"It was dated yesterday," Logan said, looking up at each of them in turn. "He must have written it just before he…"

"Well, what's it say, Logan?" Jason prompted, lifting the bottle of vodka to his mouth. He still looked shaken and a little gray, as if his blood wasn't quite making it up to his brain.

Logan's hands shook as he read Perry's letter aloud in a halting voice.

Logan,

I'm certain that by the time you read this, I will be dead. How, I cannot say. Perhaps I will be shot, or perhaps poisoned or stabbed. I've no idea how hired guns go about the business of killing these days. What I do know is that Ethan Wilder will not allow me to live much longer.

I know that Seti is with you. I know all about the curse and how true it is, Logan. Seti's curse is the reason I'd kept the sarcophagus hidden for fifty years – we were waiting for Seti to return. Unfortunately, it seems our calculations of the end date of the curse were flawed.

There were only five men on the face of the earth who knew that Seti's sarcophagus rested in the Dungeon. If I am dead, then Ethan will have had the others killed as well. There is no sense in sullying their names. I will take their identities with me to the grave.

It was our plan to capture Seti once he revived and use his blood to discover the secret of his immortality. It was our firm belief that the curse would have altered his DNA, allowing him to return to life after five thousand years. We wanted that mutated DNA for ourselves. We wanted immortality.

I understand now that I was played as a patsy from the very beginning. Ethan never intended for me - or the others - to live to see Seti returned from the dead. I wasted my life protecting a secret from which I would never profit. I gave up my family, my health, and finally, my life, for it.

I was a fool, and I am sorry that I ever agreed to it in the first place. I've ruined careers and treated people badly – you included. All I can do now is try to make amends by warning you.

Know this, Logan. Ethan Wilder will stop at nothing to get his hands on Seti. Newly awake, Seti will know little of this world. He may become unbalanced by the shock of all the changes that have occurred, or he may adapt easily. I have spent hours instructing him on history and our language, but have no idea if he actually heard or understood anything I said. Also, there is no way of telling how well he will absorb the distress of his rejuvenation. You must protect him, Logan. Don't let Ethan get him. Don't let that bastard win.

Let Seti live in the peace he could not find in death.

"It's signed 'Sincerely, Lincoln Perry,'" Logan finished.

"Wow. Ethan Wilder! That's big, Logan. Huge," Leo said. He took a swig from the bottle of vodka before passing it to Chris. "He's loaded, as in stinking, filthy rich, and he has more power than God. I'm not sure that you want to get involved with him."

"Are you kidding? This letter is Perry's confession! It completely absolves Logan of any involvement," Chris said, frowning at Leo. "This is outstanding news, Logan! We need to take the letter to the police. Perry's named his killer! It'll get you off the hook for everything!"

"Yeah, I guess I could say that it was delivered to me here," Logan said, staring at the letter he held. "After all, it was, in a way." He looked pale, and his hands were still shaking.

"Logan, are you well?" Seti asked. "Whoever this Ethan Wilder is, I will not allow him to hurt you."

"I'm fine, Seti. It's been a helluva day," Logan said, waving a dismissive hand at Seti. "First, I hook up with a guy who's older than – and until recently was just as inanimate as - dirt up to twelve hours ago, but is suddenly alive and kicking, and then the man I worked for is murdered. Now, to top it all off, I'm probably a suspect in his murder, and have a – if all accounts are accurate – rich, septuagenarian super villain out to get me. Just another day in the life of," he sighed.

"Ethan Wilder is nobody you want to mess with, Seti," Leo insisted. "He's got the kind of power that can put a real hurt on you. Look at what he did to Perry!"

Seti snorted. "I fear no one."

"Yeah? So said three-quarters of the dead heroes in history," Chris said, rolling his eyes at Seti's bravado.

"Look, this letter is Logan's best chance at completely clearing himself," Jason interjected. "Logan is right.

For all we know the police might have him earmarked as a suspect in the murder, since he was the last one to see Perry alive. Besides, you heard what Perry wrote in that letter. Wilder is going to come looking for Seti. He's probably started already. They can't stay holed up in this apartment forever. Eventually, Wilder will find them, and then what?"

"I still think it's a bad idea to go to the police. Wilder has really deep pockets, Jason. What if he has the police department in his wallet? What will happen to Logan then?" Leo argued. "We shouldn't make any rash decisions. We should at least sleep on it."

"Tomorrow then. We'll give the cops a chance to find Perry's body, gather evidence, and then decide what to do," Jason said.

Even Chris agreed. "Yeah. We need to wait at least until after they announce that they've discovered the body. We should watch the news. For all we know, there was evidence at the scene that might lead police to Perry's killer without Logan ever having to get involved."

Logan looked down at the letter he held again. "I don't know whether to pity Perry or be pissed off at him. I thought he was a bastard when I worked for him, but it looks as though I seriously underestimated him. How evil does a man need to be to wait fifty fucking years for the opportunity to kill someone you don't even know? And all for personal greed."

"The quest for the Grail has always been seductive," Chris said. "Evidently, Perry and his friends thought that Seti's blood holds the key to immortality. The secret to living forever is a powerful motivator, Logan. Historically, it's often made men do abominable things."

"Wait…" Leo said, looking at Seti askance. "You're immortal? How? Are you like a vampire or are you more like Dorian Gray? Do you need to suck blood? Or is the secret in that pretentious bit of bling you've got around your neck?" he asked, pointing to the golden torc that graced Seti's throat.

"Bling?" Seti asked, raising an eyebrow.

"Ignore him, Seti," Jason said, flicking Leo's ear with two fingers. "He's a little loopy, not to mention slow on the uptake."

"For a group of so-called scientists, their theorem was seriously flawed, anyway." Chris said, shaking his head. "They assumed Seti to be immortal, and yet planned to kill him to get the secret of his longevity. How do you kill an immortal? That's an oxymoron if ever there was one. Besides, there is nothing to substantiate the conclusion that Seti is immortal, anyway."

"He did live for over five thousand years," Leo insisted. "That's pretty fucking immortal in my book."

"He was cursed and mummified, then rejuvenated. There's a definite distinction between forced hibernation and living forever. There are no facts in evidence that support the claim that Seti can't die," Chris argued haughtily. "And unless you want to try putting a bullet in him, there's no way to prove it, either."

"Yeah? What about that little show he put on with the water from the fish tank? That wasn't computer graphic imagery, you know. No CGI that I've ever heard of leaves wet spots on the wall and floor," Leo said, nodding toward the fish tank.

"Whatever power he manifests doesn't suggest in any way that he can't die," Chris countered. "Just because Copperfield can make an elephant seem to disappear doesn't make him Peter Pan."

"There's a difference between illusion and magic," Leo insisted. "What Seti did was magic."

"Magic isn't synonymous with immortality," Chris sniffed.

Leo glared at Chris, frustrated. "You are a stubborn asshole."

"Well, that's as irrefutable and earth-shattering a scientific deduction as I've ever heard," Jason laughed. "Congratulations, Leo. You've won the Nobel. Besides, Perry's letter never once said they planned to kill Seti. Only that they planned to use his blood to discover his secrets."

Seti looked irritated as the debate raged between Logan's friends. Finally, he huffed as if exasperated then bent down, scooping Logan up into his arms. "I am weary. We will rest now," he said, turning his back on Jason, Leo, and Chris. Ignoring Logan's protests, he carried Logan into the bedroom, slamming the door shut behind him.

"Well, somebody's a little grumpy," Leo said, staring at the closed bedroom door.

"Once again you've overlooked the obvious question, Leo," Chris said, turning to look at Jason. "They're sleeping together?"

"Guess so," Jason grinned.

"Logan is such a lucky bastard," Leo sighed. "Did you get a load of the six pack Seti's got stashed under that t-shirt?"

"I hadn't noticed," Chris mumbled.

"Yeah, right. That t-shirt is tight enough for you to see his spleen, but you didn't notice," Leo said. "I was watching you. Your eyes never it made higher than his neck, and often not higher than his belly button." He sighed again. "And I'll bet dollars to doughnuts that he's not wearing underwear. Things were looking up below his waistband. Big things. Huge things-"

Chris elbowed Leo. "We get it."

"We're not, but evidently Logan is," Leo laughed.

"Getting it, I mean."

Jason and Chris both swatted Leo on the arm. "Shut up, Leo," they said in unison.

"I don't care if Logan is a prime murder suspect or if Ethan Wilder is gunning for him," Leo said wistfully, "I'd still love to be in his loafers right about now." He grabbed the vodka bottle from Chris and took another long swallow as he stared at the bedroom door.

For once, Jason and Chris could not find fault with Leo's logic. They sighed in unison, nodding in agreement. Reluctantly, Jason flicked on the television set, changing the channel to CNN and turning up the sound.

The weatherman was standing in front of a large map, talking about the next day's cold front as small, animated storm clouds drifted across it. His deep voice with its studied newscaster monotone echoed in the apartment.

"Don't you think that's a little loud?" Chris asked, raising his voice to be heard over the volume of the television. "I'm not hard of hearing and I'd like to keep it that way."

Jason cast another look at the closed bedroom door. "I have the distinct feeling that things are going to get noisy in there. I, for one, don't get my kicks by being an auditory voyeur – at least not when the moans and groans are Logan's."

Chris looked back and forth between Jason and the bedroom, then reached for the remote and turned the sound up another notch.

CHAPTER TWELVE

Ethan sat at his huge, intricately carved mahogany desk, staring out the windows at the city's lights when his private line rang. He snatched the phone from the receiver before it could ring twice.

"Speak," he said, without preamble. He listened intently as the voice on the other end of the line told him what news of Seti was to be had.

Ethan had set the detectives on Seti's trail as soon as he'd received Perry's phone call that Seti and Ashton had gone missing from the Museum. It hadn't taken them long at all to trace them to Ashton's friend's apartment.

"Are you certain of what you've seen?"

"Yes, sir," Joe said. "They're faggots, alright. There was only one man at home when Ashton and Seti arrived. They weren't in the apartment for ten minutes before the two of them went into the bedroom, took off their clothes, and did things that would peel paint. Then, this morning Ashton's other friends came in and they talked for a while before taking off, leaving Ashton and Seti alone, and the two of them got cozy again. Now their friends came running back into the apartment house like their asses were on fire."

"Where are they now?"

"In the apartment – all five of them," Joe said. "They were standing in the living room, waving their arms at each other like they were having an argument. Now Ashton and Seti are back in the bedroom.

"Oh, we got names of Ashton's friends, by the way. Thought you'd want to know. There's Jason Levy, whose name is on the lease of the apartment. Chris Sexton and Leo DeBarry are the other two guys. All of them are grad students. Levy has an internship at Sloan-Kettering. The other two are unemployed as of the moment."

"Good work."

"Boss, how much longer do you want us to wait? We could move in now, take them by surprise-"

"Do nothing until you hear from me, do you understand? Nothing. I will not risk losing Seti because you two imbeciles were impatient."

"Yeah, sure, boss. Whatever you say."

Ethan Wilder's eyes narrowed as he hung up the telephone and considered his options. Perry had been taken out of the equation. The assassin Ethan had hired was notoriously efficient and expeditious in carrying out his orders – it was his reputation for being quick and deadly that had convinced Ethan to pay the price he had demanded without question. Ethan's assassin had taken care of Perry with the same efficiency with which he'd killed the other three members of the team in Florida.

Perry's body had not yet been discovered. There had been no word from any of the moles Ethan had planted at the Museum, and there had been nothing about his murder on the news. The authorities, at any rate, hadn't yet found the body.

But where could Ashton's friends have gone, and what would have made them flee back to the apartment with such speed? Could it be that they had been nosing around in the Dungeon on Ashton's behalf? Trying to seek information from Perry about Seti? It was possible.

If they had, then they'd stumbled across Perry's remains. That presented another set of problems for Wilder. Three more witnesses who would need to be erased. Three more killings, three more significantly hefty checks that Ethan would need to write.

Ethan Wilder had not amassed his fortune by being a spendthrift. He'd already paid through the nose for four killings and had no intention of paying for any more. At least, not at the price he'd been charged for offing Perry and the others.

These were four lowly graduate students. Intelligent, perhaps, but not smart enough or lucky enough to dodge a bullet, no matter whose gun fired it. He could easily have the detectives he'd hired to snatch Seti take care of Ashton's friends at the same time, and it would only cost Ethan a fraction of what Perry's killer had charged.

He smiled, nodding to himself. One problem solved.

Ethan rose from his desk and made his way across his office to the wall-to-wall bookcase that graced one side of it. His hip throbbed as it usually did when he'd sat for too long. A hip replacement had been performed five years ago and its legacy of aches and pains was a constant reminder to Ethan of his mortality. Each twinge reminded him that death was just around the corner and that his time was swiftly running out.

Not that he'd need to worry about death for much longer.

Reaching for his leather bound copy of translations of the Egyptian Book of the Dead, he pulled it halfway from the shelf. There was a slight grinding noise before a large section of the bookcase swung open, revealing a hidden room.

Ethan grinned as he always did when he opened the secret panel. It had been an indulgence that had cost him plenty, but it had been worth every penny he'd paid and necessary in order to keep his plans secret. He always felt a bit like Indiana Jones when he slid behind the dark mahogany bookcase into the laboratory he'd had set up behind it. Perhaps a cross between Indiana Jones and Baron von Frankenstein was more apt, he chuckled to himself, eyeing the pristine counters and cabinets and the expensive, highly sophisticated scientific equipment that filled the room.

A centrifuge, an electron microscope, a titration calorimeter, a vortex mixer, a laminar flow cabinet, a state of the art mainframe computer, and myriad other shiny new toys sat covered in transparent plastic sheeting, waiting for the moment that Ethan got his hands on Seti. In the exact center of the room was a hospital bed, equipped with steel handcuffs and leg manacles.

The last, most crucial piece of equipment had yet to arrive. Ethan had retained the services of one of the best in the field of DNA research, Dr. Gupta-Patel, who had once done highly specialized, groundbreaking work with the Human Genome Project.

As soon as Ethan received the call that Seti had been captured, he would book a flight to the United States for Patel. Then the tests would begin, and Ethan would finally realize his dream. His destiny.

He would become immortal.

Ethan retreated, slipping out of the lab and closing the bookcase panel, returning to his desk. Propping his elbows up on top of the desk, he tented his fingers under his chin, staring at the screen of his laptop.

Seti.

Ethan had waited fifty years for the first glimpse of him, which had come from a grainy, unfocused digital photo emailed by the investigators.

Judging by the photo, Seti looked just like any other

man on the planet. One would never know simply by looking at him what miracles flowed in his blood, or what knowledge was stored in his memory. But Ethan knew. And Ethan had every intention of prying Seti's secrets loose by means of modern scientific experimentation.

In addition to the medical tests, Ethan planned on administering a battery of psychological tests to Seti as well - Rorschach, IQ, neuropsychological among them. Plus, there was a plethora of questions that Ethan was itching to ask Seti about the ancients. How many of the deductions anthropologists had made over the years from the evidence found in digs were true? How close had they come to envisioning life before the Pyramids?

In a very short while, all of Ethan's questions would be answered.

Then his thoughts drifted to the disturbing bit of information his investigators had relayed regarding Seti and Ashton. Ethan had never considered the possibility that Seti might want sex upon awakening - food and drink, yes, certainly, but sex? For Wilder, having been impotent for the last thirty years, sex was usually the furthest thing from his mind. The act was barely more than a dim memory and had not been a factor in his strategy.

Even if he had considered it, Ethan would certainly never have contemplated that Seti might not care which gender tended to his body's needs.

A thought suddenly occurred to Ethan that would never have crossed his mind before hearing the detective's report. Could Seti have preferred men, even before his death? It was possible, Ethan conceded. The legend had claimed that although Seti had fathered many offspring – all of which had been killed by Seti's enemies after his death in order to decimate his bloodline – he had never taken a wife. Concubines, yes, slaves, most definitely. But there had never been any mention of King Seti's queen.

With a start, Ethan realized that he'd made a crucial error in his calculations. Regardless of the gender of the lover Seti most preferred in his bed, the possibility that he'd taken one at all posed a new problem for Ethan.

Ethan had never considered the prospect that Seti might want not only want sex, but also companionship. Now that he thought about it, it would stand to reason that after five thousand years alone Seti would no longer wish to be isolated.

Seti would have remembered a life where he had owned slaves. As a king, he would have had all of even his smallest needs tended without needing to lift a finger.

Ancient Egyptians, Ethan rationalized, believed that a man continued his customary lifestyle in the world of the dead. They were buried with their riches, with everyday utensils, sometimes with their wives and slaves so that their lives would go on uninterrupted after they'd crossed over into the Underworld. Sex would have been just another task required of Seti's slaves in both life and after death.

Awakening to find Ashton waiting for him, it would only be natural for Seti to assume that Ashton had been provided to him as a personal slave by the gods.

After all, Seti had been a king before his death and mummification - he would fully expect to be a king in his new life, as well.

Not that any of it would matter after today. Ashton would be dead, along with his friends, and Seti would become a permanent guest of Ethan's by nightfall.

What Ethan did know was that if Seti had claimed Ashton as his property, he would not easily be parted from him. Where Seti went, his slave would follow. Separating them would be next to impossible.

It would be easiest and best, Ethan decided, for the detectives to go in, kill Ashton and his friends, and remove

Seti from the apartment all in one fell swoop.

Ethan picked up the phone, dialed the number and gave his orders.

CHAPTER THIRTEEN

P ut me down!" Logan yelled, bucking wildly in Seti's arms as Seti carried him into the bedroom. It was all Seti could do not to drop him on his head, and as Logan's skull came in contact with Seti's chin, jarring his teeth, Seti was sorely tempted to do just that.

"Be still!" Seti ordered, frowning down at Logan. "You need rest. I need rest. And I will not allow you out of my sight. I gave you my oath to protect you and I cannot do that if you are not with me."

"I hardly think I need protection in the middle of Jason's apartment! Who's going to attack me? The fucking goldfish?"

"You are angry," Seti said. Confusion seemed to be the normal state of being for Seti since he'd awoken. Nearly everything Logan said or did muddled Seti's brain. "Why would you be angry at me for trying to protect you?"

"Because I don't need protection! I'm a big boy, Seti. I even eat at the grown-up's table now. It's insulting for you to insinuate that I can't take care of myself, picking me up like some errant toddler who needs a time-out and carting me off!"

"I do not understand half of what you just said," Seti grumbled, depositing Logan on the bed. The truth was that he didn't understand half of anything Logan had ever said. "I am weary," he said, deciding to dismiss the entire conversation rather than continue to argue. Besides, trying to follow Logan's convoluted logic was giving Seti a headache. Things were much more uncomplicated before. Seti commanded and everyone else followed his orders without question. Simple.

He was discovering that things were not so straightforward here, in this age. Here, everyone seemed to have an opinion, and showed no qualms about sharing that opinion with all and sundry, without being asked. Talking one over the other until their words merged into a cacophony of confusion. It was entirely too chaotic an atmosphere. Seti felt exhausted simply by listening to them all.

Stripping off his t-shirt, he tossed it to the ground. Seti noticed that Logan's eyes opened a bit wider as they gazed as his bared chest, and Seti hid a grin as he flexed his muscles for Logan's benefit. "Are you not tired?"

"A little. But a 'Hey, Logan, how about a nap?' would have sufficed. You didn't have to turn into Conan the Barbarian and drag me off by my hair!"

"I do not know who this Conan person is, and I did not touch your hair." Seti replied as he slowly hitched his sweatpants down over his hips, stepping out of them. Seti's grin broke the surface, watching Logan's cheeks pink as he sucked his lower lip between his teeth, his gaze lingering at Seti's groin.

Logan's tongue might be angrily wagging, but the rest of his body gave Seti every indication that his mind was not on the argument.

"Logan..." Seti whispered with longing, leaning down over the bed. He braced himself over Logan with one arm on either side of Logan's head. Happily, Logan didn't twist away, although he planted his palms against Seti's chest. "Logan, I want you. I need you. Do you not want me?" he breathed, barely touching his lips to Logan's. Each word was a tiny caress against the soft flesh of Logan's lips. "Did I not make your body writhe with ecstasy? Do you not wish to feel that way again? I will make you scream your pleasure, Logan."

"Kind of stuck up on yourself, aren't you?" Logan asked, but his voice was very soft and husky, and he did not pull away, Seti noticed. "Arrogant. Conceited. Egotistical..."

"Enough talk," Seti said, pressing his lips firmly against Logan's. Petal soft and warm, giving easily under his own, they tasted as sweet as the grains they'd eaten that morning to break their fast. Seti's tongue hungrily pushed past Logan's lips, sweeping in like a conquering army.

To his surprise – and discomfiture - Logan did not lie still, placidly accepting Seti's attack. He refused to surrender control to Seti, his behavior more like a brave and seasoned warrior than a bedmate. Logan's tongue met his thrust for thrust, every bit as bold and forceful as Seti's. It was battle for dominance, and for the first time in Seti's life he contemplated allowing himself to be defeated.

The thought had never occurred to him before, but when it did it was shocking, unsettling, and curiously seductive.

What would it be like, Seti wondered, to have Logan command him, to have Seti's control wrenched away and be forced to submit to another's will? To lie passively underneath another man while he took his pleasure in Seti's flesh? Not to rule, but to obey?

Seti shivered as a sudden, delicious thrill raised gooseflesh on his skin. He had never surrendered before. He had never trusted any lover enough to give them that gift. Not even with Ashai had he conceded his dominance. Seti was a king in life; he was no less than one in bed. Even in his most private moments Seti had ruled his universe with an iron fist.

But now Seti found himself wondering and wavering, seriously considering the idea. The dominant within him bellowed indignantly against it, warring with the new, inquisitive Seti that struggled to surface, the part of him that ached to allow Logan intimacies Seti had never before permitted anyone. To lie still for him as he worshiped Seti's flesh with his hands and tongue. To allow Logan to breach Seti's body and ride him hard, until he left Seti gasping and spent.

The very idea went against his grain. Seti felt the notion abrading his ego like the rough desert sands, and yet the temptation to allow Logan his head grew stronger with each passionate thrust of Logan's tongue, each nip of his teeth, each stroke of his hands across Seti's back.

Even as he waged his internal battle, his hands kept busy, pulling at Logan's clothing. Seti's need was great – whether he would take or be taken was yet undetermined, but the desire to feel Logan's naked skin next to his was irresistible.

Bared at last, Logan's flesh was warm and smooth, an expanse of hard planes and sharp angles that beckoned to Seti like an oasis in the desert. His cock filled, pressing against Logan's thigh; Seti's mouth watered for a taste of his silken skin. Each second that he denied himself the pleasure increased his desire until Seti's body trembled with want, the urge to thoroughly ravish Logan nearly overpowering him.

Yet the tantalizing temptation to roll over, bare his underbelly in submission, still danced within Seti's mind, and he vacillated.

Seti's body finally made his decision for him. Stretching out on the bed next to Logan, Seti lay flat on his back with his hands at his sides. His fingers twisted in the sheets as if to keep him bound to the bed. "Take me, Logan. Do what you will with me," he growled through clenched teeth.

Seti's dark eyes sparked as he fought against his nature, struggling to keep still as Logan rose up over his body, straddling Seti's thighs. Looking up at a man was a new perspective for Seti, one that he'd experienced only when in his youth, on the very rare occasions that an opponent had gotten the best of him during battle training.

He fully expected Logan to seize the unprecedented opportunity Seti had presented him with, lift Seti's knees high and take him hard and fast before Seti could change his mind.

Instead, Logan leaned down and kissed him, a soft, sweet kiss.

"This is hard for you, isn't it?" Logan whispered, looking Seti in the eye.

"You are hard for me," Seti answered through gritted teeth. He couldn't decide if he had meant Logan's body, or his company. Or both. Submission, compounded by talking, was nearly too much for him to bear. All he knew was that his mind was screaming at him to take back control, while his body was begging for Logan to do more than talk.

"Tell me the truth, Seti. Before, in your old life, you didn't bottom, did you? I can tell. It's as if you're waiting for me to attack you, rather than make love to you. You're lying there as stiff as a board."

"This is stiff," Seti growled, thrusting his cock upwards into Logan's belly. "Attack me or please me, the choice is yours, but do not make me wait any longer."

Logan gasped, swearing softly under his breath. With his next breath he claimed Seti's mouth in a brutal kiss that tasted of claiming, of ownership. The ferociousness that had blazed in Logan's eyes a few moments ago returned, burning brightly and matching the growl that rumbled in his chest.

Seti imagined that he could feel Logan's kiss all the way down to the soles of his feet. It heated his belly and hardened his cock painfully, a groan escaping his lips. Everything faded away, even the memories of five thousand years captive in his tomb with nothing but the faintest lingering scent of sandalwood to keep him company. All that existed in that moment was the tongue that mercilessly swept his mouth, and the hard, lean body that teased his flesh with its closeness.

His fingers strained, digging into the mattress. Every muscle tensed, every nerve in his body electrified as Logan's lips finally left his, freeing him to breathe.

Except that suddenly Seti found himself unable to do so. How could he possibly perform so mundane a task as breathe while Logan's fiery lips were blazing a trail across his chest? Suckling at his breast, delving into his navel? How could he force his lungs to function while Logan's soft, wet tongue painted random patterns across his stomach, or those teeth nipped at the delicate flesh of Seti's inner thighs? When his warm breath ghosted over Seti's cock?

The edges of Seti's vision grew dark, shadows creeping in. Luckily, Logan saved Seti the embarrassment of a faint when he chose that moment to close his sweet lips over the head of Seti's engorged arousal. Seti's involuntary gasp drew a deep, ragged breath into his lungs.

Oral sex was nothing new to Seti. He had always enjoyed it, but this…this was something else entirely. Logan was not merely pleasuring Seti with his mouth – he was worshiping him with it. Enthusiastically. Masterfully.

Logan's hand pulled back Seti's foreskin as his tongue swirled around the organ's head, dipping and teasing at the tiny slit at its center. It flicked under the ridge, traced the thick vein that ran its length. Teeth nipped at the delicate skin, not enough to hurt, but enough to pull a groan full of ache and need from Seti's throat.

His mouth slipped lower, sucking Seti's furred sac between his lips, rolling the stones over his tongue as his hand stroked Seti's rigid shaft from root to tip.

By the time Logan returned his attention to Seti's cock, Seti had forgotten his pledge to keep his hands at his sides. They threaded into Logan's soft hair, holding Logan's head immobile as Seti's hips thrust his cock upward into the warm, wet mouth. Logan took him in eagerly, easily, hungrily. Wet noises added to Seti's pleasure, the music of lovemaking adding fuel to the fire that burned in his groin.

Logan's fingers massaged Seti's inner thighs, kneading at the knotted muscles until they relaxed. Seti spread his legs a little wider, wanting more contact, needing more. Logan rewarded him by slipping a finger down, tracing the root of his cock backward to the tiny opening that lay between Seti's cheeks.

No one had ever touched Seti there before, not even Ashai. Seti would never allow it. He'd protected his entrance fiercely, refusing to allow anyone to breach his body.

But for Logan, he spread his legs even wider, bending them at the knee. His body tensed when the tip of Logan's finger pressed against his hole, rebelling at the thought of being taken. His cheeks squeezed together, trying to guard it, to keep out any intruders. Logan did not miss the reluctance, and raised his head, looking at Seti questioningly.

"Seti, if you don't want this, we don't have to…"

"I want. I need," Seti growled, more at himself than at Logan. "Touch me," he ordered. With a jerk, he spread his legs even wider, staring up at the ceiling, his brow knit, muscles tense.

Logan's soft chuckle brought a flush of indignation to Seti's cheeks. But before Seti could chastise him for laughing at what Seti considered a supreme sacrifice, a single finger slid deeply into his body. It crooked within him, hitting a part of him Seti hadn't known existed.

A wave of unexpected pleasure rippled up Seti's spine, making his belly clench and his balls swell even more. Fire erupted in his groin, a delicious inferno that burned and sizzled, raising the hair on Seti's arms and legs. A moan reached his ears, low and needy. He barely recognized his own voice and was shocked in the pleading that escaped his lips.

"More, Logan. Please," Seti groaned, writhing and trying to push himself further down onto Logan's finger, even as his hips tried to push his cock upward into Logan's sweet, hot mouth.

He felt his body stretched as another finger joined the first, both curling within him. Great Ptah! He'd never known, had never dreamed being taken could feel like this. The pleasure was nearly more than he could bear.

Then Logan's fingers and mouth were gone. Seti felt their absence sharply as a sudden aching emptiness in the core of his being. Before he could protest, something much larger, much hotter than Logan's fingers pressed against his hole, seeking entrance into his body.

Seti looked down between their bellies, watching Logan's cock begin to sink into his body. He felt the burning pain of it, the stretch that made Seti fear being torn asunder.

But his body gave way, opening to allow Logan's length entrance. It slid within Seti to the root. Seti's eyes rolled back into his head as he was doubly assaulted – by Logan's flesh and by the uncanny feeling of connection that he'd felt the first time they'd made love.

"Logan," he moaned, sliding his palms over Logan's chest, toying with the nipples.

Logan began to move within him in long, leisurely strokes, brushing that spot deep inside his body each time, pushing Seti closer and closer to the edge. Logan's fingers wrapped around Seti's cock, stroking it in time to his thrusts until Seti pounded his fists against the mattress, his back arching from the bed. Tendons bulged in his neck as he twisted from side to side, losing himself in a superheated orgasmic explosion unlike any he could recall experiencing before.

No one had ever drawn such a sharp climax from him, so powerful that it bordered on pain. So overwhelming that Seti had no awareness of Logan achieving his own; Seti wasn't conscious of Logan adding his own heated puddle of seed to Seti's, streaking his abdomen and pooling in his navel. He didn't hear Logan's cries of joy, indeed, barely heard his own. All Seti heard was the rush of blood thundering in his ears; all he felt was the cataclysmic shattering of his core as he was flung toward the stars.

It was Logan's warm, soft lips kissing him tenderly that he first became aware of as he floated back into himself. Seti wrapped his arms around Logan's back, pulling the man flush with his body, their quickly softening cocks nestled together between them. "I will never let you go, Logan," he breathed. "You are my life. You are my heart."

Logan didn't reply, instead kissing him again and rolling to the side, snuggling close. Within minutes, he was asleep, Seti following shortly after.

CHAPTER FOURTEEN

I am hungry."

"You? I'm the one who should be starving," Logan said, the corners of his mouth lifting in a cheeky smile as he laid his head on Seti's shoulder. "I must have burned more calories than a marathon runner."

Seti's dark eyes, still sleepy and sated, turned toward him. "You did well," he said. "For a stripling," he added after a short pause, smirking.

"Stripling? Are you saying that I'm too young for you?" Logan asked, cocking an eyebrow. "Well, you can't blame me for that. You're the one robbing the cradle, mister."

Seti laughed, a deep, contagious rumble. "I fear that there is no one on this earth who would not be an infant compared to me."

"You've got a point, I guess," Logan grinned. "Come on. We napped, and now I feel like pizza."

"Who is this Pizza, and why should you feel like him?"

"Not who...what. Pizza is a what. It's food - delicious, crusty, gooey, cheesy, mouthwatering deliciousness. The food of the gods of the twenty-first century, delivered right to your door. It doesn't get better than pizza, my friend."

"Ah. Then I feel like pizza also."

Logan laughed again, leaning in for a quick kiss. "Get dressed. I can't wait to see your face when you take your first bite." He slipped out from under Seti's arm and scouted the floor for his clothes. He darted around the room, pulling each article on as he happened across it. Logan finished dressing before Seti had even rolled out of bed. "Come on! I'm famished!"

Seti grumbled, but obeyed. Logan stood stock still as Seti swung his long legs over the side of the bed and stood up to his full six-foot-four. Even though Logan had twice tasted every inch of the yards of delectable flesh that covered Seti's long bones, he was still overwhelmed by the sight of Seti naked.

His shoulders were nearly twice again as broad as Logan's own, his arms bulging with unconscious strength. If tested, Logan thought that Seti could probably tear him in two without breaking a sweat. His chest was deep, his stomach ridged with ropy muscle. Lean hips and long, powerful legs tapered to elegantly arched feet.

Although Seti's cock was softened from their recent play, Logan's inner eye flashed with the memory of it as it had been fully engorged. It was a cock worthy of a king, he thought, biting his lower lip.

The only flaws on Seti's body that Logan could see were a few thin, white scars marring the expanse of his sleek, toffee-colored skin. One high on his left shoulder curved, following the contours of the muscle. Another slashed along the left side of his ribcage, and yet another sliced diagonally across his left thigh. Smaller scars, some so faded that they could barely be discerned, were scattered here and there. Small imperfections, they did little but serve to heighten one's awareness of Seti's beauty.

Each scar, Logan was sure, had a story to tell. Someday, Logan thought, when he could finally look at Seti without instantly achieving a hard-on that left him consumed by lust and panting with desire, his brain reduced to its most primal state, he might actually retain enough presence of mind to ask Seti about them.

Even now, so soon after an orgasm that had drained him and left him teetering on the point of idiocy, Logan's cock twitched as his eyes feasted themselves.

"Food," Seti reminded him. There was a small, conceited smile playing at those lips that made Logan realize he'd been staring. Again. He wrenched his gaze away with an effort, feeling his cheeks heat. Damn Seti for his arrogance! And damn me for getting suckered in every time I look at him, Logan thought.

Still, Logan couldn't help himself. Seti was far and away the most physically beautiful man Logan had ever seen in the flesh, even if his mannerisms were sometimes like fingernails on a chalkboard to Logan's nerves. Seti did things to Logan that before had only existed to him in the category of "physical impossibilities," like multiple orgasms and a cock that refused to lie down and behave itself, even after just having had sex.

"You really need to get over yourself," Logan mumbled, tossing Seti his sweatpants.

Seti grunted, still smirking, stepping into the pants and drawing them up to his waist. Logan felt a pang of remorse even as a part of him felt relieved. It was for the best. If Seti remained nude much longer, Logan was apt to become mesmerized by his nakedness again and they'd both starve to death. He led Seti out into the living room, where Jason, Leo, and Chris were settled together on the sofa, watching a re-run of I Love Lucy.

All three of their faces wore identical grins as they turned toward Logan and Seti. Logan knew in an instant that he and Seti had been overheard. Not that they'd made any attempt at being discreet – as a matter of fact, Logan distinctly remembered them being quite vocal. He cringed inwardly as he recalled screaming things as he came that normally would have made his ears bleed. Still, the three of them didn't need to take such obvious pleasure in his embarrassment.

"Shut up," he snarled before any of them could open their mouths. "Not a word, any of you."

Seti's attention was caught by the television set. He'd hunkered down in front of the screen, tapping his fingers against the glass, trying to get the characters' attention. Logan watched his face darken as Lucy and Ricky blithely continued their conversation, paying him no heed.

"You're wasting your time. It's not real, Seti. They're moving pictures, that's all," Logan tried to explain before Seti tried to break through the screen and strangle the Ricardos for ignoring him. "They can't see or hear you."

Seti stood, glaring at the television set. "If they are not real, then what purpose do they serve?"

"Entertainment," Leo said. "Didn't you have that back in the Stone Age?"

"He's not a Neanderthal, Leo," Logan bristled.

"Close enough for government work. I believe I remember him throwing you over his shoulder and carting you off to have his wicked way with you," Leo retorted, grinning mischievously.

"He didn't throw me over his shoulder," Logan protested.

"Oh...he just had his wicked way with you then?"

"Shut up," Logan said, at a loss for a better come back. After all, Leo was right – on all counts. "I promised Seti pizza."

"Wow, the man works cheap. Wonder what I could get for a Big Mac and a shake?" Jason laughed. Leo and Jason high-fived each other, while Chris shook his head and rolled his eyes at the two of them.

"Just ignore them, Logan. You know that they never matured past middle school," he said.

Logan took Chris' advice. He picked up the phone and dialed the number of their favorite pizza parlor and placed an order for three large pies with the works.

He sank down to the floor next to Seti and gave him a crash course on the history of television. Logan grabbed the remote, flipping through the channels, trying to explain how a television functioned.

"What is this?" Seti demanded, snatching the remote away from Logan. He shook it next to his ear, listening intently, then turned it over in his hands, looking at it from all angles. His thumb hit several buttons, changing the channel and setting the volume to max.

"LET'S GET READY TO RUMMMMMMMBLE..."

"Wrestling," Logan yelled, prying the remote from Seti's fingers and lowering the volume. "It's fake, too."

"No, that is real. I know battle training when I see it," Seti growled, pointing at the screen. "This is how we trained our warriors, also." He squatted down, watching the nearly naked wrestlers for a few minutes. "They must be your mightiest warriors. Why do they not wear clothing like this?" he asked, plucking at the material of his sweats. "Am I not as fierce a warrior as they? They understand that clothing such as this restricts movement. I do not like being confined. "

"They are wrestling in a ring, and are dressed appropriately. You are sitting in a living room, watching television. There's a difference," Logan argued.

"I think Seti's right," Leo grinned impishly. "Take 'em off, Seti. Show Logan who's boss."

"Knock it off, Leo!" Logan hollered, shooting a black look over his shoulder at Leo. "Stop egging him on!"

Logan was spared a battle of wills between himself and Seti when the doorbell buzzed. "Thank God. The pizza's here," he said, standing up, digging his wallet out of his pants pocket. "Man, when they say 'delivery under thirty minutes,' they mean it."

"Yeah," Leo said. "God forbid they should have to take a couple of bucks off your bill. Better that they run over blue-haired old ladies in their walkers getting it to your door on time."

Jason went to answer the door. He'd just slid open the deadbolt when the door exploded inward, sending him flying backward against the wall.

Two men burst into the apartment, both with guns drawn. "Hold it right there!" one of them shouted, swinging the muzzle of his gun in an arc. "Don't fucking move!"

"Who are you? What do you want?" Logan yelled, backing up a step. He tossed his wallet at the man's feet. "Here. That's all I've got. Take it and go!"

"Stupid asshole. We don't want your money. We want your friend," Harry growled, taking another step into the apartment. "Where's Seti?"

"That's him, over there on the floor," Joe said, motioning toward Seti with his gun. "You! Get up! Put your hands on top of your head and keep 'em there."

Seti rose gracefully to his feet. "These are not your allies, are they, Logan?" he asked quietly. There was ice in his voice that made Logan shiver, despite the pounding of his heart.

"Don't move, Seti. They have guns," Logan warned Seti, not taking his eyes off the two intruders. "They can kill you."

"These insignificant maggots?" Seti laughed, stepping in front of Logan. "I have seen more dangerous piles of camel dung."

"Stop right there," Harry warned. Aiming his gun at Seti, his free hand withdrew a pair of handcuffs from his pocket. He tossed them at Seti's feet, where they landed with a loud clank. "Put those on him," he ordered, waving the muzzle of his gun at Logan. "Now! Move!"

"Come on, man... You don't need to do this," Chris said. He and Leo stood by the sofa, frozen in place. "He's a nobody. You don't want him. You must have the wrong apartment. His name is Ted. He's a dancer at The Men's Shop. You know, that new club downtown?"

"Nice try. Say something else so I'll have an excuse to shoot your faggoty ass," Joe snarled at Chris, pointing his gun at Chris' head.

Logan saw Jason eyeing the first gunman. "No, Jason, don't!" he yelled just as Jason lunged for the gun.

A shot rang out, sounding impossibly loud in the small apartment. Jason gasped, clutching at his stomach. Looking down, his face turned a ghastly greenish-white. Slick, dark blood seeped between his fingers, soaking into his shirt, dripping to the carpet. Groaning, he slumped back against the wall, slowly sliding down to the floor.

"NO! JASON!" Logan shrieked, adding his scream to Chris and Leo's. He tried to brush past Seti to reach Jason, but Seti was as immovable as rock.

"You dare bring war to my doorstep?" Seti bellowed, his face twisting into a mask of rage. Raising his arms, he called out in a language Logan didn't recognize. The windows of the apartment began to shake, as if being battered by a strong wind. In the next heartbeat they shattered, glass swept inside the apartment by a powerful gust. Howling, the wind whipped through the room, knocking Chris and Leo to the floor.

The fish tank tipped over, its water cascading over the table in a waterfall to the rug. But instead of soaking into the carpet, the wind picked the liquid up, swirling it through the air.

Incredibly, the wind and water began to take on a

form, a diaphanous bubble that quickly divided in two, like an amoeba. A pair of creatures, made entirely of water and wind and vaguely reminiscent of wolves, took shape. They growled as they slunk next to Seti, chests low to the ground, ears back and teeth bared.

Guns blazed as Joe and Harry pumped several rounds at the terrifying wind-wolves. The bullets passed harmlessly through the watery beasts, lodging in the floor and wall behind them.

A strong hand held Logan back as Seti nodded toward Harry and Joe. "Kill them," he said simply.

Logan watched from over Seti's shoulder as the wind-wolves leapt at the intruders. Snarling, snapping their jaws, they pounced on the men, knocking them both to the ground.

Harry and Joe's screams were gurgled as watery jaws snapped down on their throats, crushing their windpipes. They thrashed beneath the creatures, their arms and legs passing through the beasts without any effect.

It was over quickly. As soon as Harry and Joe stilled, the water-wolves exploded into a spray of water that soaked the bodies. The wind calmed until the only sound was that of the televised wrestling match and Logan's heart as it pounded in his ears.

The intruders lay side by side just within the doorway, their bodies completely unmarked. Wide, unfocussed eyes stared at the ceiling; their mouths open in frozen, silent screams. It looked as if both had simply dropped dead in their tracks.

"Jason!" Logan cried as soon as he could find his voice. He didn't know how Seti had conjured the creatures that had killed the intruders and he took no time to wonder about it. Not when his best friend was lying on the floor near the door, his life's blood oozing out of a bullet wound. Logan pushed past Seti, dropping to his knees next to Jason. "Oh, God," he whispered, looking at the blood that soaked Jason's shirt. "Oh, God... Jason..."

Chris was the first to gather his wits about him. He had the phone in his hand and dialed 911, barking their address into the receiver.

Leo sunk slowly onto the sofa, his face a pasty white. His hand covered his mouth, his eyes riveted on Jason.

Logan paid neither of them any mind. His attention was focused solely on Jason. Blood dripped from the corner of his mouth, and his breath gurgled wetly.

"There's so much blood!" Logan groaned, his voice brittle with grief. "Fuck! This is all my fault! I should never have brought Seti here. I should have never gone snooping in the Vault to begin with! Oh, God, Jason, I'm so sorry!" he wept. "Don't die on us, Jason. You hear me? Don't you fucking dare die!"

"The ambulance is on the way," Chris said, as he knelt next to Jason. "This isn't your fault, Logan. It's Ethan Wilder's fault. He's got to be the one behind this – he's the only one who would know who Seti is and that he'd be with you."

"I'll fucking kill that bastard!" Logan sobbed. Strong hands hooked under his arms, pulling him up from the floor despite his protests, and he found himself cocooned in Seti's arms. "No, let me go, Seti! I have to help Jason!"

"You cannot help him now, Logan. He has begun his journey to the Underworld," Seti said softly. "May Anubis guide him safely to his new life. May Osiris find his heart worthy of eternal happiness."

"NO!" Logan screamed, struggling to be free of Seti's embrace. "No! It can't be! He can't be dead!"

Chris' face looked stricken as he glanced up at Logan and nodded slowly.

Grief and guilt tore a hole in Logan's heart and a ragged scream from his throat as the pain of Jason's death seared him. Hot tears flowed unchecked down his cheeks as he buried his face in Seti's neck. "Why Jason? He didn't have anything to do with this! It's my fault! I should be the one who's dead, not him!"

"It is the will of the gods," Seti answered. "I am sorry I could not protect him."

As Logan trembled in Seti's arms, his grief quickly gave way to a terrible, numbing blackness that filled him. It was his fault. It was Seti's fault. It was Ethan Wilder's, Perry's, and God's fault. It was everyone's fault but poor Jason, yet he was the one who'd paid the ultimate price.

Outside, the wail of an ambulance and police cars drew near. Blankly, Logan watched Chris step over the dead gunmen, ready to wave the paramedics and police into the apartment. Wrenching himself away from Seti, he said, "Go into the bedroom, Seti. The cops can't find you here – you don't have any identification. Don't let them find you."

"I will not leave you," Seti said, shaking his head.

"You don't have a choice. I have to...take care of Jason," Logan said, his voice tremulous. "He needs me."

"Logan, do you not understand that he is dead?" Seti asked in a soft voice.

"Don't say that! Don't! He can't be dead. He's hurt, that's all. They'll fix him, right? Leo, tell Seti that they'll fix him!" Logan yelled, looking wildly at Leo for his support.

Leo shook his head, his face pale and wet with tears. "Seti's right, Logan. He's gone, buddy."

"Oh, God!" Logan cried, sinking to his knees next to Jason again. "How? He was only twenty-four years old! How can he be dead? Oh, God, it is my fault – all of it!"

"Logan, come on. It's not your fault. Chris is right -

you didn't kill him," Leo said.

"I might as well have pulled the trigger. I should never have taken the job as Perry's assistant in the first place. Then I wouldn't have found Seti, and none of this would have happened."

"You cannot blame yourself, Logan," Seti said, reaching for him. "In war, men die. That is the way of it."

"This isn't war! At least, not Jason's war! Not Chris' or Leo's or mine! It's only you they want," Logan said. His brows knit. "But that's all it is to you, isn't it? War? And war is just a game you're used to playing, right? Death means nothing to you, does it?"

"Logan, you are upset," Seti said, pulling Logan to his feet again. "Come, we will-"

"Of course I'm fucking upset, Seti! My best friend was just murdered! Don't make this harder on me than it already is," Logan hissed, shoving Seti hard. His anger, fueled by his fear and pain, bubbled up through the grief, aimed at the one nearest him. "This is all your fault! We were fine until I got involved with you! Get away from me!"

"Logan- "

"Get the fuck away from me, Seti!" Logan cried, wrenching his arm free from Seti's hand. "Don't fucking touch me! Just leave me alone!"

Logan watched Seti back away, his expression confused as he walked into the bedroom, closing the door behind him. Logan turned back toward the door, his chest hitching as his gaze fell on Jason's body.

Logan was completely consumed by his grief, not realizing that he was moving until he found himself at the feet of the dead gunmen. Bending down, he picked up one of the guns. It felt inordinately heavy in his hand, cold metal that matched the iciness that gripped his heart. He stepped over the bodies into the hallway.

"Logan? Where are you going?" he heard Chris ask. Fingers clutched at his sleeve, pulling him back. But Chris' voice sounded far away.

Logan turned, looking at Chris blankly. Chris' lips were moving but he couldn't make out the meaning of the sounds. The gunshot rang so loudly in his head, over and over again, along with the words dead, Jason is dead, that he wanted nothing more than to clamp his hands over his ears until it stopped.

He jerked his arm free from Chris' hand and kept walking, out of the apartment and down the stairs. Shoving the gun into his pocket, he made his way to the service entrance at the rear of the building and slipped outside.

CHAPTER FIFTEEN

It should have been a minor annoyance, no more irritating than the bite of a flea.

The barest twinge that should have unnoticed in the vast, thickly crowded expanse of Setekh's memory. As a god who had existed since nearly the Beginning, his memories were piled one atop the other in stacks so dense and high that he had nearly forgotten most of them. It was a tiny, insignificant ripple that should only have been acknowledged in the deepest level of his subconscious, if that. Certainly nothing that should have disturbed him.

A curse, laid long ago and forgotten, had been broken.

Setekh had cast thousands, perhaps millions of curses during the course of his existence, in every shape and form imaginable. Boils, drought, famine, disease, and a host of other horrors had been laid on one human's head or another for their failings. At times, Setekh had cursed entire populaces into oblivion. The breaking of one of the plethora of curses he'd cast should not have caused him even minor distress.

And yet this particular twinge did not escape his notice. It bore upon it the mark of a man whose ancestors had been honored by Setekh, gifted by him, and who had worshiped Setekh in return. A man who, although he bore Setekh's name, had flouted his esteemed heritage and had defied Setekh. One who had sought to turn the very powers given him by Setekh against the god.

Seti.

Setekh's eyes blazed a bright, fiery red, his muscles tensing as he remembered the human sorcerer. How he had stood against Setekh, belligerent, arrogant, refusing to accept Setekh's will. Daring to seek revenge. Even now, after five millennia, the audacity of the man still rankled.

He rose from his throne, stalking through the alabaster and marble halls of his palace, his long, crocodilian jaws snapping in irritation.

Setekh's palatial residence rose high into the air like a glittering white jewel, a collection of exquisite, gleaming white domes, parapets, balustrades and arches. The palace's beauty was at odds with the hideousness of its King, belying his vicious and unpredictable nature. Aside from his magnificent home, there was nothing beautiful or peaceful about Setekh, god of chaos and disorder.

The finest rugs, hand-woven in brilliant jewel tones, cushioned his feet. Bowls of rare, fragrant flowers lent their delicate fragrance to the air. Golden ewers of rich, sweet wine and platters of juicy, red meat graced his tables in a never-depleting bounty. Draperies and bedding of the softest, sheerest silk and the finest linen draped his couches. Music drifted in low, soft notes throughout the air from the flutes and lyres of Setekh's musicians. Beautiful women and handsome men lay on couches scattered throughout Setekh's halls, ready to slake his lust at the crook of his finger.

And yet, surrounding his palace of dazzling opulence and splendor was a dismal and noxious landscape that stretched in every direction for as far as the eye could see. Bleak and inhospitable, the Underworld's harsh, unforgiving landscape made a sharp contrast to the beauty of Setekh's palatial abode.

Stepping outside the palace onto the broad steps, Setekh's nostrils were at once assaulted by the reek of decay. Foul and viscous water, the color of blood, flowed in a river of death that wound its way through the bleak and barren landscape in a lazy ribbon. Its banks were piled high with the bones of those who had not managed to successfully navigate the dangerous journey through the Underworld to the palace of Osiris to be judged.

Only after Osiris had weighed their hearts against the Feather of Purity would a man or woman be judged worthy or unworthy. If the scales were balanced, then the penitent would be rewarded in paradise, the riches accumulated in life following them into their new existence. If the heart weighed heavy, its owner would face an eternity of torment, his soul eaten by Ammut, Devourer of the Dead. Those who did not complete the journey but fell by the wayside, ceased to exist all together. Their ka disintegrated into ashes, scattered by the hot wind, their bodies torn apart, fodder for the beasts of the Underworld.

Those who had been properly buried, whose organs had been removed and stored in canopic jars and their bodies mummified, who had the proper spells and prayers, might secure the assistance of Anubis to guide them on their journey.

Those who did not took their chances.

Setekh heard the hissing of the crocodiles that nested on the river's banks, fearsome creatures, larger and more deadly by far than any that swam the Nile. Snakes, beetles, jackals, and all manner of loathsome beasts prowled the waist-high grasses that spread from the river like a cancer, choking the land.

The wind that blew was searing hot and malodorous as heavy, black storm clouds thickened in the red sky, pulsing with lightning. They were Setekh's contribution to the hell-spawned landscape. The storms were his children. His servants.

A scream split the air, drawing the crocs from their nests. Water boiled with the resulting feeding frenzy. Fresh meat, Setekh thought, another pathetic soul succumbing to the dangers of the journey into the afterlife.

Weak, as Setekh himself had once been.

He cursed himself for his weakness and howled, shaking the very foundations of his demesne. He should have cursed Seti for eternity rather than a mere five thousand years. The limit had been reached. Seti had awoken, returned to life and its many pleasures.

"Setekh? What's got your thong in a knot this morning? You're making enough noise to wake the dead." Osiris chuckled. His voice, as smooth as silk and as cool as water from a deep well, reached Set's ears from afar, echoing in his mind. "Get it? Wake the dead," he said. "I crack myself up sometimes."

Osiris had taken an unfathomable liking to human pop culture of the twenty-first century. He sprinkled his vocabulary liberally with references whenever possible, especially since he knew that it nettled Setekh. "Please tell me that a human isn't the reason for this little tantrum, Setekh."

Setekh met Osiris' comments with a wall of silence. Unfortunately, that was enough to give Osiris his answer.

"Ah, so it is a human. Really, Setekh. You never change. You've always let them get under your skin."

"He bore my name. I made him a king among his kind and he repaid me by taking my gifts and throwing them in my face!"

"Oh, hell, no! Are we talking about Seti? Again? I thought you cursed him!"

"I did."

"Let me guess – you didn't make the curse permanent. You put a time limit on it, and now it's up, right? Honestly, Setekh, you never think things through," Osiris chided.

"This matter does not concern you, brother," Setekh grumbled. He returned to the Main Hall, slumping down onto his throne. He gripped the arms of the throne until his knuckles whitened as he struggled to contain the fury that rose within him.

"Sure it does, brother. Ever since you expedited my way into the afterlife, I've made your business my business."

The gentle jibe at their history together only served to fuel the rage that had been steadily building within Setekh's heart. It had been a misunderstanding that caused Setekh to murder his eldest brother Osiris, and Osiris well knew it. Setekh's wife, Nephthys (a cold-hearted, scheming bitch if ever there was one), had seduced Osiris by taking the form of Osiris' wife, Isis. Infuriated by what Setekh perceived to be Osiris' betrayal, Setekh had killed and dismembered his brother, scattering the pieces.

It had taken Isis a good long while to find all of the pieces and put Osiris back together again. Then Osiris had been given rule over the Underworld, and his revenge on Setekh had been ongoing ever since.

Osiris knew that Setekh had been deceived, but still he had never let Setekh forget the incident. He had forced Setekh to live with the consequences of his actions ever since, barring him from ever stepping foot in Paradise. Setekh had been bade build his palace - while as opulent as any other god's - amid the horrors of the Underworld, where Osiris had decreed he live for all time.

"This is my affair, brother," Setekh replied, failing to keep the bitterness out of his voice. "I will see to it as I deem fit."

"You've already 'seen to it.' This particular human has been punished enough for whatever crimes you think he committed against you. He's paid his dues, Setekh. Did his time. Let him live his life in peace," Osiris chided. "Don't make me go Rambo on your ass."

Setekh growled, his eyes blazing. "Yes, Osiris," he hissed through gritted teeth. Every muscle in his body clenched, protesting his acquiescence. But Setekh knew better than to oppose his powerful brother – at least openly. What he did when Osiris was otherwise occupied was another story.

"Why do I not believe you?"

"I give you my word that I will not touch Seti," Setekh said, his eyes narrowing. "He will be free to live out his days in whichever way he sees fit." And so he would. There were other ways to cut a man, ways that would leave him bleeding and broken without ever having been touched, and Setekh was an expert in all of them.

He had done it before.

He could do it again.

Would do it again.

For the first time since realizing that the curse he'd laid on Seti's head had been broken, Setekh smiled.

CHAPTER SIXTEEN

Logan strode purposefully along the city streets, although his mind churned in turmoil. He found himself standing at the entrance to one of the most easily recognizable buildings in the city. Seventy-two stories of glass and steel, the Wilder Executive Tower rose as a sleek black monolith, an obsidian spear driven deep into the heart of the city.

Logan barely remembered leaving Jason's apartment building, or crossing any of the busy streets to arrive at Wilder's doorstep. Everything since the shooting was a blur, a maddening maelstrom of petrifying fear, white-hot pain and smothering guilt. Logan bore the weight of his emotions like a man staggering under a burden so heavy that it threatened to drive him to his knees at any moment.

The only thing that kept him upright was his rage.

Black and as sharp as a razor, his anger dwarfed everything else he was feeling. Fury at Wilder, at the gunmen, at Seti, and most of all at himself, disallowed rational thinking, allowing only one thought, vague and shapeless but nonetheless consuming, to emerge.

Revenge.

Logan narrowed his eyes and slipped his hand into

his pocket, fondling the cold, blue steel that weighed it down. It was the same gun that had taken Jason's life. Logan would see to it that it took another before long – that of the man who was ultimately responsible for Logan's pain. He had no set plan in mind, just an overriding need to deliver justice, to avenge, to share the pain that filled him to overflowing.

He glanced up and craned his neck trying to see the top of the building. It seemed to stretch forever, the upper floors barely visible from the ground. Somewhere up there, in that black tower, sat the man whose soul was stained with Jason's blood.

Wilder.

"I'm coming for you, you bastard," Logan whispered. His voice sounded like a stranger's to his ears – low, gravelly, and filled with a hate that up until today Logan would have sworn he was incapable of harboring.

"Hey. I'm Jason. Welcome to Freshman Hell. Got any weed?"

The ghost of Jason's voice whispered in Logan's head, catching him off guard. His breath hitched as fresh tears burned in his eyes, remembering their first meeting. Had it only been six years ago that Logan had walked into the dorms on his first day in college and found that he was to share a room with a towheaded young man with a shit-eating grin and a photographic memory?

Jason had been happy to show Logan the ropes of college life. He'd taken Logan under his wing, helping him find his classes, showing him where the library and the cafeteria were located in the maze of the university's buildings and pathways. Helped him to register, to figure out which classes Logan needed to take that semester.

Then, later that same semester, "You're gay, aren't you?"

Logan had become aware of Jason's sexuality shortly

after meeting him. Jason was out publicly; never once trying to hide who he was from his new roommate. Logan admired that, lusted after that freedom, but was still too deeply in the closet to admit that he shared Jason's choices.

Outing himself to Jason had been difficult, but it had also been a blessed relief, the first time ever that Logan could remember being comfortable with who he was.

Logan remembered that day fondly. The sex had been quick and fun, with no strings or demands on either one of them. Playful, and just a little embarrassing; they'd laughed about it afterwards. It hadn't been the hardcore, heart-stopping, overwhelming passion that he'd felt with Seti, not by a long shot. But the memory meant a great deal to Logan nonetheless.

It was the first and last time he and Jason had been intimate, but it had paved the way for a friendship that had endured since, expanding to include Leo and Chris. The four of them were inseparable. Had been inseparable, he reminded himself with another sharp pang.

As much as he loved Leo and Chris, Jason had been Logan's best friend. It was Jason who Logan confided in, who he'd confessed his crushes to, and who'd held his hand when his heart had been broken. It had been Jason who Logan had turned to in times of need, and who Logan had thought to go to when he realized that he needed a place to hide with Seti.

Now Jason was dead because of him.

Again a crush of guilt threatened to buckle Logan's knees. His eyes welled with tears of sorrow and rage, his throat constricting with them as his memories of Jason danced through his mind. Logan gritted his teeth against the pain, yanking open the front door of the Wilder building and marching inside.

His first obstacle came in the form of a beefy security guard with a flat top crew cut and a belly that was more keg than six-pack. The material of his blue uniform shirt stretched tightly across his gut as he sat behind a sleek, modern reception desk. Behind him was a bank of elevators, their golden doors framed in dark, burnished wood.

"Help you?" he asked Logan, flicking his eyes up from the newspaper he'd been reading. His tone suggested that Logan must be lost, since no one who looked like Logan did could possibly have any legitimate business inside the Wilder building.

"I'm here to see Ethan Wilder," Logan replied. The name tasted like poison on his tongue, and he resisted the urge to turn his head and spit.

"You got an appointment?" the guard asked dutifully, but doubtfully.

"He'll see me. Tell him that it's Logan Ashton. Tell him that I've got something for him. From Seti," Logan replied, adding under his breath, "and from Jason."

"Look, kid, if you're trying to sell him something, Mr. Wilder will have your balls for breakfast. Why don't you try across the street at the Trump Tower?"

"If Wilder finds out that I was here and that you sent me away without calling him, it'll be your balls being served with his cream of wheat and orange juice, not mine," Logan growled.

The guard grunted and shrugged. "It's your funeral, kid," he said, picking up the phone and pressing a couple of digits with a thick forefinger. He spoke quietly into the receiver. Logan caught his name and Seti's before the guard fell silent and his eyes widened, a flush creeping up his neck.

"He'll see you, Mr. Ashton," he said, setting the phone down in the receiver. "Come with me, please."

Whatever Wilder had said to the guard had made an

impression, and the use of a salutation with his surname was not lost on Logan. The guard was almost reverential, leading Logan past the desk to the bank of elevators. He pressed the button, ushering Logan inside, removing the set of keys that jangled at his sizable waist. Selecting one, he inserted it into a keyhole below the floor buttons on the elevator panel.

"This will take you straight up to Mr. Wilder's penthouse," he said, backing out of the elevator. "Look, I'm sorry I gave you a hard time," he apologized as the doors slid shut and the elevator began to glide silently upwards. Logan had no idea what threat Wilder had made to the guard if he let Logan leave, but the man sounded as if he might pee his pants.

Logan kept his hand inside his pocket, his fingers curled around the cool, comforting metal of the gun. For the briefest moment a new worry surfaced as he rode the elevator up toward the penthouse. Logan had never shot a gun in his life.

"Don't be stupid," he chided himself. "You're a college graduate. You've got your degree. It's a simple piece of machinery. You can do this. Point and shoot." He had no more time to doubt his abilities as the elevator stopped with a slight jerk and a gentle chime announced that he'd arrived at his floor.

The doors slid open, revealing a plush outer office. Logan whipped the gun out of his pocket, swinging it in a wide arc and trying not to think about how badly his hand was shaking.

Then he remembered Jason and how he'd looked like a discarded marionette laying on the floor of the apartment, drenched in blood. Logan's hand steadied even as his expression darkened.

The outer office was empty. Logan stepped out of the elevator onto carpeting so plush that he felt like he'd sunk in it up to his ankles. Burnished mahogany molding accented rich, cream-colored walls. Heavy, Victorian-styled furniture was scattered in neat, tasteful groupings, dominated by a receptionist's desk that had probably cost more than Logan made in a month. Three flat-screen monitors sat on the desk, dark.

A pair of enormous double doors stood sentry at the far end of the room. There then, Logan thought, is where his quarry lie - the lair of the beast. Shh, he thought, stifling a hysterical giggle that threatened to bubble up past his lips. I'm Elmer Fudd, and I'm huntin' millionaires.

Above the doors, a tiny blinking red light drew Logan's attention to the closed circuit camera poised above the jamb. He grunted, resisting the urge to hurl profanities at Wilder through the magic of television, since he was certain that he was being watched. His face crumpled into a scowl as he strode toward the doors.

They opened before he could reach for the handle. Silently swinging inward, they revealed an immense space much larger than the outer office. From the threshold, Logan could see clear through to the other side of the room and out into the city through the ceiling to floor windows. To his left, Logan saw a deadly array of weaponry hung for display. Axes, swords, scimitars, daggers, and spears, all antiquities, were affixed to wall plaques and gleamed under spotlights.

"Mr. Ashton. Do come in," a cultured voice called to him in a clipped, British accent. "I've been expecting you."

Logan's head snapped to the right. There, seated behind a desk that dwarfed the one in the outer office, sat a cadaverous old man. Sharp features on a skull tightly wrapped with skin bore the mark of his advanced age, his hair was snowy white and neatly styled. A dark blue suit that had the look of money hung on his thin bones. An arthritic, liver-spotted hand waved Logan deeper into the office.

He was not what Logan had expected. In his mind, Logan had demonized Wilder, envisioning him as a fanged, scaly monster with the blood of the innocent dripping down his chin. Outwardly, Wilder looked like a harmless old man, someone's grandfather. Then Logan looked into Wilder's eyes and saw the truth of him.

There was nothing grandfatherly about Wilder. His eyes sparked with intelligence and fiery fanaticism. Logan could see the snake coiled just behind Wilder's eyes, ready to strike and sink venomous fangs into Logan's flesh.

Logan's hand rose, pointing the gun at Wilder. "You bastard! You sent those assholes after me and now Jason is dead because of you! You killed Perry, too. Why? Before I do the world a favor and put a bullet between your eyes, tell me why!"

"Why? I should have thought you'd have figured that out by now, Logan. I'd heard that you were a clever young man. Tsk, tsk. Sadly, it seems reports of your intelligence were sadly overrated."

"Tell me why!" Logan roared, his finger itching to pull the trigger and blow Wilder's pompous ass into the next world.

"Why, Seti of course. Surely you've realized by now that he's special. Unique. And he is mine. I discovered him. It was my money that brought him here, that greased the palms of customs officials to get him in, and paid to keep his existence a secret from the world. He belongs to me."

"Seti is human! He doesn't belong to anyone!"

"Seti is most assuredly not human. In his veins flows the secret to immortality! That secret would have been mine by now if it weren't for you, you insignificant worm! You nearly destroyed my life's purpose!" Wilder screamed. His eyes darted to a spot just behind Logan.

Suddenly the press of cold metal touched Logan's temple. His eyes shifted to the right, meeting those of a man who'd snuck up silently behind Logan while his attention had been focused on Wilder. A bodyguard, perhaps, or another hired killer. Either way, Logan realized he was a dead man if he so much as flinched.

Ice loosed Logan's bowels as the grim realization that he'd failed sunk in. A large hand snatched his gun away from him, pocketing it. Logan forced himself to look back at Wilder, wanting beyond anything else to smash the supercilious smile from Wilder's face.

"Truly, Mr. Ashton, you didn't think me so much a fool that I'd allow you to waltz into my office and kill me, did you? You must be more of an idiot than Perry had taken you for being," Wilder said, shaking his head. "I knew the moment you arrived that my detectives had failed to procure Seti and that you were here for some sort of misguided, poorly planned revenge. Where is he?"

"Fuck you!" Logan snarled. If they were going to kill him, then so be it. He wouldn't give Wilder any information. He would take that small victory with him to the grave.

"I am through playing games! WHERE IS SETI?" Wilder roared, standing up behind his desk. The barrel of the gun pressed painfully into the side of Logan's head. "I'll find him anyway, Logan. My finances will allow me to comb this city, even if I need to do it door by door. I will find him. You might as well simply tell me, and I promise that your death will be swift and painless. Withhold the information, insist on one more minute of this false bravado, and I'll see to it that you suffer for as long as humanly possible before you die." The icy black look in Wilder's eyes told Logan that he meant every word he said.

It didn't matter. Logan's lips whitened, clamping shut into a tight, thin line, even as his heart hammered in his chest.

"Shoot off something non-vital," Wilder instructed his henchman with no more emotion than if he was ordering lunch. "Perhaps a finger or a toe. Let's see if pain will loosen his tongue."

Suddenly, the air conditioning went haywire, or so it seemed to Logan. The room's temperature dropped swiftly, the sweat that covered Logan's skin chilling him. His breath ghosted in small puffs of fog in the rapidly cooling air. Wilder had noticed the change, too. His wild eyebrows knitted together in a frown as he glanced at the vents in the ceiling.

Near the window wisps of smoke curled, thickening, taking on a shape. For the briefest moment, Logan dared hope that it was Seti, exhibiting yet another unbelievable, incredible power. But the shape that took form was much too large to be him. Its head brushed the fifteen-foot ceiling of the room as it solidified.

A giant with a crocodilian head, long jaws lined with wickedly sharp teeth, its eyes burning red, surveyed the office, locking on Logan.

A huge, clawed hand lifted, and the man who'd held Logan at gunpoint was suddenly flung across the room. His gun discharged into the air, the bullet whizzing by Logan's head so closely that he could feel the breeze part his hair. With a crash, the man hit the wall hard, crumpling to the floor.

"SETI IS MINE!" the creature, man, beast, whatever it was, thundered. It disappeared before the echo of its voice rumbled away.

Taking Logan with it.

CHAPTER SEVENTEEN

The police, a squad of uniformed and suited men with many whirring and clattering machines – Seti had no idea as to their use, nor did he care – descended on Jason's apartment like ants, crawling over everything, barking orders. Standing in the bedroom, cloaked in a spell that kept him unseen by the prying eyes that searched Jason's apartment for evidence, Seti's patience began to fray.

He'd gone too long without Logan in his sight. How could he protect Logan if he could not see the man? Right now, at this very moment one of the hard-eyed police-warriors might be questioning Logan, frightening him, touching him.

The thought of anyone but Seti touching Logan for whatever reason sent a bolt of white-hot jealousy whistling down Seti's spine, stiffening it. No one touched Logan. No one. Logan was his.

Seti gritted his teeth and did what he was best at. He endured.

The moments ticked by with maddening slowness. Not even the ages Seti had spent locked in his sarcophagus had passed with such excruciating deliberateness. Surely a sorcerer was at work here. It was the only explanation Seti could come up with to explain why time had stopped.

Finally, a face he recognized slipped into the room with him.

"Seti?" Chris whispered, peering into the darkened corners of the bedroom. "Are you in here?"

"I am here," Seti answered, remaining unseen. He watched Chris jump at the sound of his voice with no visible body attached to it. It would have been quite comical, if Seti's nerves hadn't been strung tight with worry over Logan. "Are the warriors gone? Where is Logan?"

"The who?" Chris asked. "Oh, the police! No, they're still here. Listen, Seti, I managed to duck in here, but they'll miss me in a minute. Logan is gone."

"WHAT?" Seti roared, becoming visible in the blink of an eye. He towered over Chris, every muscle in his body tensing. "What do you mean, gone?"

"He...he took off just before the police got here. I didn't get a chance to tell you before now. I don't know where he went, Seti. But he took a gun with him," Chris said hurriedly. He cast a glance at the bedroom door. "You need to get out of here, now. The cops will be back here any second – they probably heard you. Hell, the entire east coast probably heard you!"

Seti tipped his head back and howled, shimmering again into near invisibility. All that could be discerned of him was a subtle shadow, obvious only if one was looking for it.

A heartbeat later two police officers burst into the bedroom, guns drawn. Spotting Chris, a plainclothes detective demanded, "Who were you talking to?"

"A mummy," Chris answered, a little too sarcastically. His reply didn't sit well with the detective. He grabbed Chris' arm and roughly manhandled him out of the room, while the other officers searched under the bed and in the closet for whatever had made that inhuman bellow. Not finding anything, they left, closing the door behind them.

A new emotion, one Seti had never felt before, took hold of his heart in an icy vice, squeezing the breath from Seti's chest.

Fear.

Logan was gone, out in the world, unprotected. Seti had failed at his vow – again. The knowledge put his entire body on edge, each nerve screaming in protest. His sleek, dark brows knitted together as his face turned to granite, his resolve firming anew. He had lost Ashai. He would not lose Logan.

Stalking to the window, he drove his bare fist through the tempered glass, shattering it, and stepped through onto the narrow ledge outside. Ignoring the blood that dripped from his split knuckles, he raised his arms to the sky, lips moving soundlessly.

The wind responded to his call at once, a gentle zephyr that caressed Seti's skin like the soft lips of a lover.

Seti concentrated, drawing upon the magick that flowed in his blood. His body filled with a power he hadn't felt since the ill-fated night five millennia ago when he'd unleashed the fierce power of the desert winds upon his enemies. He would turn this city inside out, tear it apart brick by brick if necessary, to find Logan. He would not fail again.

The hair on his arms and legs stood on end as the air around him crackled, and his eyes glowed eerily with the potency of the power he summoned as he spoke two words into the whispering wind.

"Find him."

At once, the wind whipped into a gale. From the open ocean waters across the harbor that surrounded the city, the wind drove huge waves crashing against the shore, rocking even the mightiest of freighters moored at the docks as it screamed in across the water in response to Seti's order. With the speed of a nuclear windstorm it pushed through the city, sweeping across every inch of it.

It whistled underneath doors, howling through apartments and offices, shooting through ventilation and elevator shafts. Nothing could stand firm against the onslaught. The wind lifted park benches and garbage cans into the air as it blew through the streets, turning them into projectiles, hurling them blocks away. Hot dog and pretzel vendors' umbrellas were pulled free from their carts and sent soaring into the sky. People were knocked to the ground, sent skidding across the pavement by its force. Trees were stripped of their leaves; many uprooted altogether when they failed to bow to the tempest.

And the wind searched.

It slipped into the tiniest crevices, slammed against solid walls until it found – or made – cracks with which to enter. Every room within each building, every rooftop and basement was touched by the powerful gusts. Every vehicle, every office, every restaurant was scrutinized by the gale.

At Jason's apartment, police radios crackled to life, spurring the officers to temporarily abandon their investigation, racing to the street in response to the unexpected hurricane-force winds.

In the Guggenheim, precious canvases flapped against the walls, or were ripped free, sent flying; sculptures fell clattering to the ground. Alarms sounded but went unheard under the monstrous roar of the wind.

On Broadway, a million lightbulbs burst in a rain of glittering glass as the wind tore them free from the marquees. Posters were ripped from the walls, shredded, and sent flying through the streets. Heavy velvet stage curtains blew and twisted as if they weighed no more than gauze.

On Wall Street, the pits in the Stock Exchange were covered in a snowstorm of paper and ticker tape. In the banks, the snow was green as the wind whipped money from the tellers' drawers, sending it sailing through the lobbies.

In Fulton's Fish Market, the fresh tuna and cod that lay on beds of ice swam through the air as the wind over-turned the carts and booths.

In the penthouse of the Wilder Executive Tower, the wind paused. It swirled and eddied over the thick carpet-ing, caressing the mahogany desk and the old man who sat slack-jawed behind it. Picking up a trace scent of the one its master had bade it find, the wind withdrew.

Across the city, the wind suddenly died. Garbage and airborne debris crashed to the ground, suddenly bereft of the strong unseen arms that had held it aloft. All across Manhattan, people dodged a rain of wreckage that fell to splatter across the pavement. In the absence of the wind's thunderous voice, the silence in the streets was deafen-ing.

A single, whistling breeze blew back to the apart-ment house where Seti waited on the ledge like a flesh and blood gargoyle. Caressing his cheek, it imparted the knowledge it had gleaned from its visit to the Wilder Ex-ecutive Tower.

His face hardened with determination as Seti again called to the wind. This time it bore Seti up from the ledge and into the air. As if he rode an invisible chariot, his wind horses charged forward, bearing him west, high over the streets of the city.

Arriving at the black tower where Logan's scent had been caught, Seti faced the windows that looked into the penthouse, hovering in the air seventy-two stories above the ground. Within, he could see two men, one old, with the look of shock etched onto his face. The other was lying in a heap on the floor, unmoving.

Logan was nowhere to be seen.

Raising his hands palms-up, Seti concentrated. Above the city, black clouds gathered, belly-heavy with rain. Thunder boomed, reverberating in Seti's bones.

Then the atmosphere crackled, sending tendrils of electricity rippling over his skin as a bolt of lightning answered Seti's command. It speared down from the clouds to hit the window of the penthouse. The bolt didn't smash the glass – it melted it, 50,000°F of concentrated heat reducing the tempered glass into its original liquid form. The glass fell in a sheet, dripping down the side of the skyscraper, quickly cooling into a layer of pseudo-ice.

The wind carried Seti forward, depositing him neatly inside the penthouse. Three steps brought him to the desk, where the old man blinked up, looking at him, an expression of awe replacing the shock on his face.

"Seti? You have come to me at last!" the old man said. His face broke into a satisfied grin.

"I've come for Logan. Where is he? Speak quickly, old man, or your next breath with be your last," Seti growled. His fingers curled into tight fists, the warrior in him wanting to smash the answer out of the old man. He restrained himself by the barest of margins. Likely as not, one blow would kill the old man and Seti would never learn of Logan's location.

"Tell me first," Wilder said, either too arrogant or too stupid to realize that Seti hung on to his control by the slimmest of threads, and in no mood to barter. "Tell me what I need to know to become immortal. Give me a sample of your blood, and I'll tell you what I know."

"You will tell me now!" Seti thundered, slamming both fists down on top of the enormous mahogany desk that separated him from Wilder. The wood trembled, a yawning crack snaking across the burnished top.

Wilder jumped, falling back into his seat. He stared at the cracked desk, then slowly looked up at Seti. His face quickly lost its superior expression, dissolving into a look of pure fear. "I...I don't know where he is," he squeaked.

Seti balled his fists, ready to pound some sense into Wilder, even if it killed the old man. By that point, he was beyond caring. His temper broke free of the restraints with which Seti had kept it chained and he was again the fearsome warrior-king of ancient Egypt. Wilder must have seen his own murder shining in Seti's eyes, because his tongue loosened and he began to babble.

"He was here. Logan was, but then he left. Or rather, he was taken. Whisked away by a god with the head of a crocodile. Setekh, would be my guess. He said you were his. Where he took Logan is beyond me. Really, I swear it!" Wilder cried, flinching away from Seti.

Seti clenched his teeth, scowling fiercely. "Setekh," he hissed, spinning around and addressing the empty office. "Have you not plagued my life enough? Have I not paid for my crimes a thousand – nay, five thousand times over?" He turned his rage-blackened visage on Wilder. "When this is over and I have reclaimed the one who is mine, I shall return, old man. You have brought pain to my House. I vow to return the favor."

He turned away, stalking to the far wall of the penthouse where Wilder's collection of antique weapons hung. He ripped a bejeweled dagger off the wall, running the pad of his thumb over its lethal blade, watching a bright red line of blood well up.

There was only one way Seti knew of to follow Setekh to his palace in the Underworld.

Picturing Logan in his mind, Seti gripped the hilt with both hands. Raising it high over his head, he plunged the dagger down in an arc, deep into his heart.

CHAPTER EIGHTEEN

White hot pain clouded Seti's vision, an agonizing red fog drifting in from the edges, blinding him, driving him to his knees. When it finally cleared, he was no longer in Wilder's office.

With one quick stroke of a bejeweled dagger, Seti had proven that he was not what Ethan Wilder had thought him to be. Seti was mortal, and now he was good and truly dead.

Wilder's dagger was gone. No wound marred his chest, no blood stained his skin. He knew that his corporeal form lay crumpled on the floor of Wilder's office, still and lifeless. Seti had passed through the Veil, the power of death giving solidity to his ka.

All around him for as far as he could see, wind rippled a vast, bleak grassland of tall, brown, withered stalks. Foul and hot, the wind that blew here did not remember him; it blew against his skin with the indifferent brush of a stranger. Above him stretched a strange, blood red sky in which bloated, black thunderheads loomed. The air felt oily, heavy, the stench of death thick upon it.

The Underworld.

His threats to Wilder had been empty ones. There would be no return to life for Seti, and worse, he knew that because he had been less than pure while alive, his ka would weigh heavy against Osiris' feather. He was doomed. Ammut would eat his soul and Seti would never see Paradise.

So be it, he thought. His death was far overdue anyway. He should have made this final journey five thousand years ago. Seti set his jaw. He would complete the mission he had set for himself and then accept his fate.

Logan was not dead. He had been brought to the Underworld before his time, taken with his lifeforce still intact. For Logan, the return to life was yet a possibility, and Seti was determined to see to it that he was sent back to where he belonged.

"Welcome, traveler. Here begins your journey to your destiny. I am the Guardian of the Veil." A voice spoke that was so deep it seemed to reach the marrow of Seti's bones as well as his ears, drawing Seti out of his thoughts.

Nearby a tall, muscular creature clad in the royal apron and headdress of the ancient Pharaohs appeared. His nemes, the headdress of royalty, was of linen, and held back from his forehead by a wide gold band. Wrapped snuggly around his waist, his shendyt, the traditional Egyptian apron, was accordion-pleated in the style of the kings and as white as snow. Both made a startling contrast to the creature's smooth, blue-black skin.

"Anubis…" Seti breathed, inclining his head to the black, jackal-headed god who stood before him. "I humbly beg your help."

"As do all who pass through the Veil from life into death," Anubis rumbled, a trace of humor threading his voice. "But I may only guide you. You alone must show the courage and strength to survive the journey."

"I fear nothing," Seti replied, lifting his chin defiantly. His eyes met those of Anubis, unflinching, although the god's eyes glowed red, sparking with otherworldly power.

"Great Anubis, there is in your demesne one who does not belong here, stolen by Setekh while his flesh was warm and his heart still beating. I followed him, seeking to return him to the mortal realm. I would travel to the palace of Setekh, rather than that of Osiris."

Anubis nodded. "I am aware of this spark of life in the Valley of Death. I scented his lifeforce the moment he passed through the Veil." Anubis leaned close to Seti, his canine nose delicately sniffing the air. "I will allow this. You are strong. I can smell the blood of Kings that runs in your veins. Be strong, Seti. For you. For him."

Again Seti inclined his head, crossing his arms over his chest in supplication to the god. "I am ready."

"The dagger with which you ended your life is returned to you," Anubis declared. He held out his hand, the ornamental dagger resting on his palm, its blade stained with Seti's blood.

"I am in your debt, my lord," Seti said. Not for the first time since he'd awoken, Seti wished he had his old, familiar weapons - his scimitar, wickedly sharp and curved, and his bow and arrows. The dagger was as a child's toy compared to them, but it would have to suffice. He was grateful that Anubis had granted him any weapon at all.

"Follow the river," Anubis said, waving his hand. The tall, brown grass parted, showing Seti a glimpse of a river of blood winding through the fields in the distance. "Its waters will lead you to the palace of Setekh. Be ever watchful. The creatures of the Underworld are everywhere, and they are always hungry."

"My thanks, my lord," Seti said. Gripping the haft of the dagger tightly in his right hand, he took off at a trot through the grass in the direction of the river.

Logan's scream was still pouring out of his throat at full volume when the world tipped away. When it finally stopped spinning, Logan blinked in confusion, finding himself standing in the middle of a spacious, white room with high ceilings and beautiful, symmetrical arches.

Beneath his feet, the gleaming marble floors were covered in thick woven rush mats. The fragrant air tickled his nose with the exotic scents of sandalwood and myrrh. Alabaster walls were decorated with richly colored paintings and carved hieroglyphics. Absently, his mind began to translate them as his eyes wandered over the engraved images, although some of the figures were unfamiliar to him.

One panel bore Setekh, the god of Chaos and Disorder, and his brother, Osiris, locked in battle. The next panel pictured Setekh again, strewing pieces of his brother's body to the four winds. In a third panel, Setekh was portrayed eating what appeared to be Osiris' penis – literally, and sans the rest of him.

Gruesome, Logan thought. There's some nice, brotherly love going on there. A sound caught his attention and he turned. At the head of the room was a raised dais, flanked by life-sized statues of the god of the earth, Geb, and his wife, goddess of the sky, Nut. Between them was a throne that would have been the envy of any king in history. Solid gold, accented with strips of creamy ivory, the throne was inlaid with precious gems. Emeralds, diamonds, and rubies, some the size of ostrich eggs, sparkled in the light of the torches that lit the room.

Seated on the throne was a statue of Setekh, in all his crocodilian glory.

At least, Logan thought it was a statue, until it moved.

"How pathetic humans are," Setekh said, waving a hand at Logan. "Weak. Fragile. Breakable. The reek of mortality clings to your skin."

"How did I get here?" Logan sputtered, eyes wide as he stared at the monstrous form of the god who had cursed Seti.

"So, you are Seti's new plaything," Setekh continued, as if Logan hadn't spoken. Logan could feel the oily touch of Set's gaze as it crawled over his body, and shivered. "You are not much to look at. Mayhap you have other talents that are not obvious to the naked eye. Show me your hidden gifts and perhaps I will allow you to live a while longer."

Jaws full of long, sharp, yellowish teeth parted in a parody of a grin as Setekh moved aside his loincloth, baring a penis that was thick, fully erect, as big around and as long as Logan's forearm.

"Um, I'd rather not," Logan said, backing up. "Where in hell did you take me? For that matter, why did you take me? I have nothing you'd want!" A fist of fear wrapped itself tightly around Logan's heart, squeezing. If this was a nightmare, then it was the most realistic one Logan had ever experienced. He could actually smell Setekh's hot, rank breath, and feel the cold that emanated from him in waves.

"I want because Seti has," Setekh replied. "He deserves nothing, and nothing is all I will allow him! You belong to me now. And when he comes for you, I will destroy him!"

"What did he ever do to you? He's only human. You're a fucking god, for God's sake!" Logan yelled, anger masking his fear. His muscles tensed to the point of snapping as instinct readied his body for fight or flight - flight being Logan's first choice. "Wasn't cursing him to five thousand years of being buried alive enough?"

Setekh bolted from his chair, his penis bobbing obscenely. "He dishonored me! He dared carry my name and abuse my gifts!" Setekh's roar thrummed in Logan's bones, making his teeth chatter. "He deserves nothing but pain and endless sorrow for his disrespect and ingratitude!" Setekh stamped down a foot that caused a small tremor to ripple though the palace.

Logan's eyes grew round at the godly tantrum Setekh was throwing - he was acting like a toddler denied his own way. Logan half expected Setekh to throw himself on the floor, kicking and screaming and banging his fists, holding his breath until he turned blue. Gulping, Logan wondered who in the universe was big enough and strong enough to give this particular monstrous infant a time-out.

"What makes you think Seti will follow me? How could he, even if he wanted to? This is the Underworld, isn't it? It's not as if the Afterlife has an off ramp on the interstate." Logan's eyes darted from side to side, looking for an escape route. He turned and spotted an archway behind him that opened onto an endless sea of grass.

Logan turned on his heel even as Setekh's mouth opened to reply, and made a dash for the doorway. He hadn't gone far when he hit what felt like an invisible, immovable stone wall, bouncing back. Logan landed hard on the rush mats, the wind knocked out of him.

Setekh's laugh was as grating in Logan's ears as broken glass. "Foolish human, you are most amusing. Surely you do not think you can escape me?"

Logan groaned, pushing himself up to a sitting position. He scrambled backwards as Setekh took a step toward him. "Seti won't follow me. You're wasting your time!" he shouted. "Stay away from me!"

Logan cringed as Setekh stalked forward, looming over him. One large, clawed hand reached for him, thick fingers encircling Logan's throat. Logan's hands pounded at the fist that choked the breath from him and lifted him bodily from the floor. He hung suspended in the air, feet kicking ineffectually at Setekh's hard body. Gray spots floated in from the corners of his vision as his lungs labored to breathe.

"You belong to Seti. He claimed you - I can smell his seed on you. He will come to reclaim what he believes to be his." Setekh's eyes sparked malevolently, narrowing to slits. His long, slimy, black tongue lapped along the side of Logan's face. "And when he does, your flesh will fill my belly."

CHAPTER NINETEEN

The going had grown more difficult when Seti reached the river. The ground near the banks of the stinking water was a slurry of thick, black mud that sucked at the soles of his feet, slowing his progress.

Cloying, the air near the river was thick with the stench of death and clouds of small, biting insects. They swarmed around Seti's face, irritating his eyes and nose. The smallest of the Underworld's predators, the mosquitoes and gnats were the first to taste Seti's blood. Swatting at them did little good – there were too many. For every one that Seti brushed from his skin, there were thousands more to take its place.

Seti drew heavily now on his warrior training, his mind racing backward through the millennia to the time when he ruled the sands of Egypt.

For a moment he saw himself in his inner eye: a youth whose chin was barely dusted with fuzz, naked save for a penis sheathe and armed with a simple wooden staff. He faced his father on the golden sands of the training arena, a man whose body bore the scars of countless battles. Kindness had been banished from his father's eyes; instead he wore the fierce expression of a warrior who would take no prisoners.

Seti's father's voice rang in the ears of his memory.

Focus on your target - nothing else matters. Be alert. Your enemy is always poised to attack. You may know not where or when he will strike.

He remembered the pain of his father's staff striking his shoulder, and the shame that had ripped through him. Seti had not been paying close enough attention, had been daunted by the size of his opponent and distracted by their familial relationship. The blow brought him to his knees.

Listen. The largest enemies may make the smallest sounds. Act. React. Do not pause. A heartbeat's hesitation is enough time for your enemy to cleave your head from your body. Do not doubt your abilities.

A swift dodge left Seti's staff striking nothing but air. He had not been fast enough, had given his opponent too much warning of his attack. Another blow, this time to his upper back, threw him facedown in the dirt.

Breathe. Scent the air for your enemies, let your skin feel for the heat of their bodies on the wind.

Seti learned many painful lessons on the training field, but they had left him a warrior to be reckoned with, and fully capable of assuming his father's crown. Added to his magical inheritance, Seti's training allowed him to become a force that had blown across the sands of Egypt, conquering everything in his path.

His bearing shifted and he stood taller, more confident as he plugged along the mucky riverbank. He was still Seti. He was still the fierce warrior he had once been.

A small, bubbling sound caught his ear and he turned to look toward the river. A ripple stirred the water a few feet out from the bank, no more than a small disturbance in the surface, but enough to put Seti on guard. His grip tightened on the haft of his dagger, pointing the sharp blade toward the water.

It came quickly, bursting up through the surface of the water in a leap that brought the crocodile nearly to Seti's feet. Its jaws gaped as it hissed, its short, thickly muscled legs quickly closing the distance between it and Seti.

Half again as long as Seti was tall, the beast's wide jaws were lined with wicked teeth. It snapped at Seti's legs, angling its head to sink its teeth into Seti's flesh. One snap would seal Seti's doom, and he knew it. The crocodile would clamp down tight, dragging him back into the water. Spiraling in a death roll, the creature would keep Seti underwater until his lungs filled with the murky, putrid liquid of the river and he drowned.

Seti was far too familiar with the behavior of crocodiles and reacted with the instinct of one born and raised among them. The Nile had been thick with them, ferocious beasts that preyed on anything and everything that they could catch. Birds, wildebeest, camels, men - even lions were not immune to the crocodile's jaws.

Moving quickly, Seti sidestepped the animal's attack and straddled the scaly monster, plunging his dagger up to the hilt into the top of its broad, flat head.

The crocodile bellowed, its body twisting violently from side to side, jaws snapping up in the air, trying to reach the blade that bit deeply into its brain. Eventually, its movements grew jerky, then stopped as the great beast slumped into the mud, lying still.

Seti worked the blade out of the crocodile's skull. If he had still been king, he would have skinned the beast and taken its teeth as trophies of his kill. But, now, he had no time for such vanities. Leaving the enormous carcass behind for the scavengers, he pressed on.

Seti had no idea of how long he walked. Time had no meaning in the Underworld. Ra would not allow the rays of the sun to touch the fields of the dead; Night, and her son, Dusk, ruled the withered plains and foul river. Without the sun there was no way for Seti to mark the passing of the day. There was only varying degrees of darkness. It felt as though he had been walking for days.

His feet blistered, his shoulders and legs ached, but he kept on. To stop, to rest, would leave him open to attack. The scavengers knew he was tiring; they were smart, staying close but just out of reach of his dagger, waiting for Seti to misstep.

A pack of hyenas kept pace with him. He could hear them snuffling in the bush, their mottled coats blending with the dried, brown stalks of tall grass.

Vultures circled above him, gliding on the air currents in slow, lazy circles. Seti could feel their sharp eyes watching him, waiting patiently for their chance to tear at his flesh with their cruel, hooked beaks.

All around him the hiss and clicks of scarabs and scorpions whirred, heard but unseen in the waist-high grasses.

Doggedly, Seti pushed on, forcing himself to move faster.

Finally, blindingly white domes shimmered into view in the distance, rising from the desolate, brown landscape like an oasis in the desert.

The sight of Setekh's palace gave Seti heart and the strength to redouble his pace. Breaking into a jog, his braids beat a rhythmic tattoo against his back with each step. Sweat dripped into his eyes, burning them, but he ignored the sting. He kept his eyes trained on the palace, not daring to look away, praying that it was not a cruel mirage.

He slowed only when the wide steps that led up to Set's palace loomed into view. Panting, he took a moment to regroup himself, to catch his breath.

The hesitation nearly cost him everything.

It came from behind him. Perhaps it had been waiting,

coiled in the deep black shadows cast by the palace, or perhaps it had tracked Seti unseen from the beginning. In either case, the attack came the moment Seti paused.

A hiss that blew hot air against the skin of his back was all the warning Seti received as a monstrous form struck out at him. Only instinct saved him from being impaled on the creature's needle sharp fangs.

He twisted to the side, throwing himself to the ground and rolling, his body responding to the threat even as his mind struggled to process the fact that he was being attacked. A flat triangular head, as large as Seti's sarcophagus had been, struck so close by that he could feel the rush of air the beast displaced with its startlingly swift movement.

Slowly, arrogantly, as if already assured of its next meal, the cobra lifted its head. Soulless black eyes watched Seti with the crafty gaze of a predator. Rearing, it towered over Seti, its body as thick around as a tree trunk. Mirror-like scales shimmered with swirls of iridescent green and gold, Seti's face reflected in them a thousand times over. The snake's fangs were each as long as Seti's forearm, and razor sharp. Strings of viscous venom dripped from each, its breath reeking of death.

The great cobra's hood rose, exposing its fierce, kohl-lined false eyes, casting dark shadows over the beast's face. A long, sinewy black tongue flicked out from between its jaws, its forked end tasting Seti's scent in the air.

Seti's fist squeezed the dagger haft tightly. He barely had time to take a deep breath before the cobra struck again, its massive head snapping toward him. Again, he rolled to the side an instant before the creature's fangs would have pierced his flesh, this time bringing his arm down in an arc. The blade of the dagger sunk deeply into the cobra's left eye.

Scrambling up and away, Seti bent low over the stairs, trying to stay out of the way of the cobra's head as it convulsed, wildly swinging, first in one direction then the other. Seti ducked and rolled, trying to keep from being crushed by the weight of the cobra's mighty head.

As the cobra's head repeatedly struck at the unyielding, cold stone steps, the tip of one of its fangs broke off with a sickening crack. It lay on the step in a small pool of translucent venom.

Arching up off the ground, the cobra twisted away into the tall grass, flattening a large swath in the crisp, brown stalks as it slithered away to nurse its wound.

Seti's heart pounded in his chest as he pulled himself to his feet. His dagger, his only weapon, was gone, still embedded in the eye of the great snake. He turned, looking up at the entrance to Setekh's temple from over his shoulder. There was no time to chase after the snake, even if the wound he'd inflicted had proven fatal and he was able to retrieve the dagger from the snake's carcass. Logan was in there, with Setekh. Seti needed to act now.

Then he spotted the piece of ivory-colored fang lying on the step near his feet. It was as sharp as any dagger, and a better weapon than none at all. Carefully, he picked it up, holding it by its blunted, broken end. Three fingers wide, as long as his hand, Seti knew that one scratch from the venom-drenched fragment would be more than enough to kill.

Whether one could kill a god was a mystery Seti did not have an answer for, nor did he want to think about the possibility that nothing he did could harm Setekh. All he knew was that he had to do something, anything to get Logan away from him.

Seti took a deep breath and ascended the stairs to the archway that led into the palace of Setekh.

CHAPTER TWENTY

S ETEKH!"
Logan struggled to remain conscious, clawing desperately at the fingers that squeezed around his throat. A familiar voice bellowed the name of the god who held him firm, but it sounded far away to Logan. Miles away. No doubt it was just his imagination trying to conjure up the one person who might have been able to save him from Setekh.

Seti.

He hadn't had enough time to get to know Seti. Logan knew that now. He belatedly realized that while he'd blamed Jason's death on Seti, it really hadn't been Seti's fault at all. The only one who could be blamed for his death was the god whose hand wrapped around Logan's neck.

As he lost his battle with consciousness, Logan's last thoughts were a wish and a prayer. A wish that he could have told Seti as much, and a prayer that Seti would find his way in the modern world. That he would be happy.

Suddenly, Setekh's fingers loosened their hold and Logan felt himself fly through the air, his back smacking hard against the wall. Gasping for air, his hands automatically massaging the bruises at his throat, he blinked at the sight of the man who stood framed in the archway that led out of Setekh's palace.

It couldn't be. He'd left Seti back in Jason's apartment. How could he have known where to find Logan? How had he managed to follow him here? And why?

Logan tried to call out, to warn Seti away, but all he could manage with his ruined throat was a weak rasp that even he could barely hear. "Seti! No!" his mind thundered, although his voice was less than a whisper.

"So, you have followed your whore-toy to my demesne," Setekh growled. Logan watched with wide eyes as Seti squared off against the much larger, omnipotent god. "I suspected that you would be foolish enough to do so. You were always weak when it came to your playthings, Seti. Did the last five thousand years not teach you that what I take, I keep?"

"You will not have him, Setekh!" Seti roared, taking a step into the room. His eyes never left Setekh, his body looked tightly coiled and ready to strike.

"I already have him," Setekh laughed. "I must compliment you on your choice of whores. He was most... accommodating." Setekh's hand slipped to caress his grotesque erection.

Damn, but Logan was getting tired of not only hearing himself referred to in third person, as if he didn't warrant first person status, but of hearing himself called a whore. "Liar!" He managed to cry, still not at full volume, but loud enough to be heard. Don't believe him, Seti, he thought, trying to gather his legs underneath him and stand up. He failed, sliding back down the wall into a heap. His body, exhausted, battered and bruised, had reached the boundary of its endurance.

Setekh's head snapped toward him as if suddenly aware that Logan was still in the room. "Silence! You have reached the limits of your usefulness, human!" He took one angry step toward Logan before Seti bellowed a chilling warrior's cry and lunged.

Logan gasped as Seti flew across the room, a sharp bone dagger in his upraised fist. "No, Seti!" he screamed, his throat constricting in protest. In horror, Logan watched Setekh tangle his fingers in Seti's braids, lifting him in the air and flinging him away in one smooth movement.

Seti hit the floor and skidded across the rush matting, lying facedown and frighteningly still. He didn't seem to be breathing. Logan felt an icy wave of fear and black desolation sweep over him. "You finally did it, didn't you?" he spat at Setekh. "You finally killed him. And why? To sooth your fucking ego? Because he bruised your pride? You're a fucking god – what more do you want? How much of a greedy bastard are you?"

Logan pushed off the wall, trying to stand again. Failing that, he began to crawl toward Seti's still form, dragging himself painfully over the floor to his side. Setekh's shadow loomed over him, and he felt Setekh's hot, rancid breath on his back before Setekh's claws dug painfully into his flesh, hauling him to his feet.

"I was going to allow you to live, little human – at least, until I had tired of you. Now your fate will be his!" Setekh roared.

Logan frantically pushed at Setekh's arms, beating on them with his fists, kicking for all he was worth, trying to free himself as Setekh's jaws opened wide, but it was no use. Scrunching his eyes shut, he held his breath and stilled, waiting for Setekh's long jaws and jagged teeth to tear out his throat.

A heartbeat passed, then another. Still another, and yet Logan breathed and his head remained firmly attached to his body. Cracking open one eye, he looked at Setekh, bewildered, not daring to hope for a reprieve from the death sentence Setekh had laid on his head.

The expression on Setekh's face was one of shock and pain. He dropped Logan, clutching at his shoulder where Seti had managed to plunge the cobra's tooth before Setekh had thrown him across the room. Roaring, Setekh spun away from Logan, cursing Seti. His bellows were earsplitting – it was all Logan could do not to cover his ears and scream himself.

Instead, he continued crawling toward Seti. Reaching him, Logan turned him over onto his back. Seti moaned, giving Logan hope.

"Seti? Seti, look at me," Logan said, laying a hand on Seti's scruffy cheek. His skin felt cold to the touch. "Seti?"

Seti's eyes blinked open. "Ashai?" he breathed.

Behind them, Setekh continued to scream, his shrieks and howls echoing in the chamber.

"No, it's me. It's Logan." Pulling Seti's head onto his lap, Logan began to rock. Suddenly, it became too much. Everything seemed to catch up at once and he felt his sanity strain at its moorings. "I can't do this anymore, Seti. Please, wake up and get us the hell out of here, okay?"

"Failed you." Seti's voice was weak, a mere shadow of its former deep, glorious strength.

"No, no you didn't. Come on, Seti, get us out of here," Logan said, shaking his head. He couldn't believe that this was the end. He wouldn't believe it. He wouldn't let Seti give up.

"No. Weak. I was weak."

Before Logan could protest again, he felt something whiz by, perilously close to his ear. The ivory fang, streaked with black gore, quivered in the floor where it impaled itself. An inch to the left and it would have bitten into Logan's left thigh.

"I am through with you both!" Setekh roared. "Your very existence is a blight on me, a pestilence, and it ends now!"

Improbable thunder rumbled, the room flashing with electrically charged streaks of lightning as Setekh raised his arms to the ceiling. His eyes glowed a fearsome red, sparking with hate. The thunder built to a crescendo that made Logan's ears ring painfully.

Time seemed to slow for Logan, each second bloating until it took up the space of a lifetime, and his vision sharpened until he could discern the fine hair on the legs of the small fly that buzzed lazily over Setekh's left sandal and count each beat of its translucent wings.

Logan's eyes darted toward Seti. His pain was painted clearly in his strained expression, shaded with fear and grief. Logan couldn't bear to see him like this, his proud and mighty warrior beaten by a bully of biblical proportions.

Something inside Logan snapped. Anger unlike any he'd ever known before, greater even than that he'd felt with Jason's death, sparked. It mushroomed instantly, like a nuclear explosion, rushing through his blood, carrying a payload of adrenaline.

As Setekh roared above them, Logan's hand wrapped around the serpent's fang that had bitten deeply into the floor nearby, pulling hard on the ivory shaft.

It pulled free. Logan pushed himself forward, his arm swinging upwards in an arc, and plunged the dagger into the heavy sac that swung beneath Setekh's monstrous penis.

No creature of the earth could have made a sound like the one that exploded from Setekh's throat as Logan twisted the fang, working its sharp, poisonous tip deeper in Setekh's scrotum. Setekh's scream filled the room like a solid entity, blocking out all other sound, even the beat of Logan's own heart as it pounded in his skull.

Setekh backed away, hands cupping his savaged groin.

"Swine!" he spat. "You will not find the path to paradise after I finish with you. Osiris will never weigh your heart, you bastard son of a pig-loving whore!" he shrieked. One long finger with a jagged, black nail pointed toward Logan. "I curse you to wander forever in the Underworld, your flesh fodder for my servants!"

"NO!" Seti cried. Logan felt his pain as if it was his own, white-hot and crippling. Seti pushed himself up and threw himself sideways across Logan's lap, as if to protect him from Setekh's curse. "Osiris!" he cried. "I beg you, help me! My soul for his! My allegiance, my life, my eternal servitude for your protection!"

"Osiris will not help you, you ungrateful son of a jackal! You turned your back on my blessings for want of this pathetic mortal! You have damned yourself and him along with you!" Setekh roared. "I am master here, not that sniveling coward, Osiris! He turns a deaf ear to those who walk my lands!"

"Enough."

The word was softly spoken, and yet cut through the din raised by Setekh's storm and howls. Immediately the thunder ceased and the lightning dissipated, the room falling ominously silent.

Turning his head toward the sound of the new voice, Logan saw a tall, bearded man, his skin an impossible shade of green, standing framed in the doorway. On his head he wore a conical crown flanked by two large black and white ostrich feathers, which Logan immediately recognized as the atef crown of Egyptian royalty. He carried a shepherd's crook in one hand and a leather flail in the other.

"Osiris," Setekh hissed, snapping his jaws at the new arrival. "This is none of your concern!"

"Enough," Osiris repeated. His voice was rich with authority; the air seemed to crackle with its power. "Setekh, you are a total pain in my ass. Dude, you really need to get a life. Metaphorically speaking, of course."

Logan blinked, staring slack-jawed at Osiris. The contrast between his ancient Egyptian appearance and his use of curiously modern slang was incongruous. Logan liked him on sight. For the first time since he'd found himself in Setekh's palace, he dared feel a glimmer of hope.

"Stay out of this!" Setekh bellowed, raising his arms threateningly.

"Bite me," Osiris snorted, pointing his crook at Setekh. A blindingly bright flash erupted from it, sizzling through the air, hitting Set squarely in the chest. "What part of 'enough' didn't you understand?"

Setekh flew backwards, his body hitting the wall behind him with such force that he cracked the sandstone. A shower of dust and debris fell with him as he crumpled to the floor. A smoldering, black scorch mark marred the skin of his chest where Osiris' bolt had hit him.

"You need to learn to play nice with the other kiddies," Osiris chided, shaking his head. "And don't think I'm going to forget the 'coward' crack, either. You are so on my shit-list." He turned his kohl-rimmed eyes toward Logan, smiling. He cocked his head, looking at the fang that protruded from Setekh's sac. "Ooh...got him right in his moneymaker. Nice shot, kid," he said, winking at Logan.

Behind Osiris, Setekh wailed, cupping his sac, his body undulating and shimmering, slowly disappearing until nothing was left but the dent his bulk had put in the wall of his palace.

Osiris smiled at Logan. "I'll deal with him later. Honestly, sometimes I don't think he has the brains Geb gave to a slug. Now, I'll just bet that you've had your fill of the fun and games down here, huh? Ready to go home?"

Logan grinned in spite of himself. "You can say that

again. You're Osiris, aren't you? The All-Father, god of the Underworld-"

"Lord of the Sky, god of fertility, yada, yada, yada. I've read the press releases, kid."

"Great Osiris," Seti moaned. He tried to sit up, but Logan kept him from moving, wrapping his arms around him tightly. "I humbly beg you to send Logan back to the mortal realm. He was stolen by Setekh. He did not pass through the Veil willingly." It was obvious to Logan that speaking was taxing what little strength Seti had left, and that worried him.

"Shh. Rest, Seti," he admonished, laying his hand against Seti's cheek. Unshaved, the bristles of Seti's scruff tickled at his palm. Turning back to Osiris, Logan said, "How about it, your...er...godship? Can you send us back?"

"You, Logan. Not me," Seti whispered. "I cannot return."

"What do you mean? Of course you can. You did it before. You're not even mummified this time."

"No, I cannot." Seti's skin paled further, dark circles discoloring the flesh beneath his luminous black eyes, the lines on his face cutting deeper into his skin. He seemed to age before Logan's eyes, wrinkles forming, gray streaking through his black braids.

"What he means is that the big lug committed hari-kari to come down here after you," Osiris said, clucking his tongue. "That's a big time sacrifice. Assures him of brownie points at the weigh-in center."

"No!" Logan cried, as the truth hit him with the force of a sledgehammer. Seti had killed himself? Over him? "Why, Seti? Why would you do something like that?"

"I swore to protect you. I failed."

"You didn't fail, Seti," Osiris said, walking – or rather gliding, over to where Logan sat cradling Seti's head. His feet never seemed to move or leave the ground. "You did protect him. If it wasn't for you, Setekh would have killed him a few minutes ago."

"He would not have been taken had it not been for me, my lord," Seti said, his eyes drifting closed. "And I have pledged you my servitude."

"No! Seti!" Logan cried. He looked up at Osiris, frantic. "Please, don't let him die!"

"Technically, he's already dead," Osiris said with a shrug. "His ka is disintegrating, assuming its spirit form. It's preparing to travel to my palace, to be weighed against the Feather of Life to determine if Seti gets the all-inclusive vacation in Paradise, or the one-way ticket to the Damnation Plantation."

"Please," Logan begged. "None of this was his fault! He deserves better than this! Didn't he suffer enough for five thousand years? Take me instead!"

Osiris rolled his eyes. "You humans are so melodramatic. Personally, I don't want either one of you. Look, I'll give you one more chance, and Seti? Don't screw it up this time." He pointed his crook at Seti and another dazzlingly brilliant streak of light poured from it. The light enveloped Seti's body from head to foot in a golden glow. It felt warm under Logan's hands, like an electric blanket set to high.

When the light faded away, Seti's color had returned, the strain and age that had shown on his face vanishing along with the heat. He took a deep breath, slowly sitting up. When he turned toward Logan, his lips curled in a warm smile that spoke volumes.

Logan grinned, his eyes burning with feeling. "I didn't mean it," he said. "What I said to you back in the apartment. I don't blame you for Jason's death. It was Gator-boy's fault, not yours."

"Gator-boy?" Osiris laughed. "Oh, I'm going to have

to remember that one. That'll get his breechclout in a twist, for sure. Speaking of whom, you'd better get going. I can't hold him forever, and he's going to have a bitch of a headache when he gets loose. You really don't want to be here for that."

"Jason," Logan said, suddenly feeling the pain of his friend's death return to weigh on his shoulders. He'd nearly forgotten. "Is he...is he here?" he asked Osiris. "He got to Paradise, right?"

"Now, that's privileged information, kid. But I suppose you deserve something for the trouble my brother caused you." Osiris smiled. "Yeah, he's made the "A" list. He's living it up big time with the party crowd in Paradise."

Logan felt a painful twinge in his chest, thinking of Jason. But at least now he knew that his friend was happy. It was more than most people got when they lost someone they'd loved.

"But, my Lord...my pledge... " Seti said, looking up at Osiris. "I traded my servitude for your help. I do not forget my oaths so easily."

Osiris laughed. "Don't worry. I'm not going to forget that either. Someday I'll give you the chance to make good on it. Until then, have a nice life. You've earned it."

The next thing Logan knew, the world was again spinning away.

CHAPTER TWENTY ONE

Logan screwed his eyes shut as his stomach roiled with the sensation of spinning, wind howling in his ears. His arms clung to Seti, aching from fighting the nearly irresistible centrifugal force that pulled at him.

Even after the whirling sensation stopped and the world stilled, his stomach protested the journey. Pressing his forehead to Seti's, he prayed that it was the last time he'd ever have to experience that particular sensation.

Logan blinked his eyes open and took a moment to take stock of their surroundings.

Plush carpeting cushioned his bruised body. The air was cool, scented lightly with citrus. They were surrounded on three sides by tall, creamy walls accented with deeply burnished mahogany trim. To his right sat a huge, imposing desk fashioned from the same rich wood.

Osiris had been true to his word. They were back, right where they'd started, in Wilder's office.

"Where did you go?" Wilder's voice demanded. A quick glance in his direction showed Logan that Wilder hadn't moved from behind his desk. His bodyguard was still slumped unconscious on the floor.

Wilder's voice was imperious, demanding an answer.

"You've been gone for hours! Seti, come here," he ordered arrogantly.

Logan ignored him completely. "Are you okay, Seti? Can you stand?"

Seti nodded, smiling at him. Together they struggled to their feet, testing muscles that had been abused during their confrontation with Setekh. Logan, for one, felt like a walking black-and-blue bruise.

"Answer me!" Wilder screeched, "I demand to know where – and how – you disappeared! Who was that monstrous creature that was here? Was that really the god, Setekh? And you, Seti! It's because of me that you've awoken, and yet you dare use my own dagger to end your newly restored life? Come here, I said!"

"Shut. Up. You've caused enough trouble for one day."

Logan turned toward the familiar voice. Osiris stood near the immense windows of the office, backlit by the setting sun, staring pointedly at Wilder. "What?" he asked, glancing at Logan, the picture of innocence. "I couldn't just plop you back up here to deal with my brother's mess, now could I?"

"Who are you? I demand some answers before I call the police!" Wilder shrieked. His hand fell on the telephone receiver. "I'll have you all arrested! I'll-"

"Please. I'm shivering in my little pharaoh booties," Osiris said, waving a dismissive hand at Wilder. "I'd really think twice about making that call. Have you forgotten what you've done? Let's see...kidnapping, conspiring to commit murder...oh, yes, and let's not forget grand theft on an international scale. After all, the sarcophagus you illegally dug up and smuggled out of the desert fifty years ago was really the property of Egypt, pal. Interpol is going to love that."

Wilder's face blanched an impossible white as he

slumped down into his chair. "You can't prove any of that," he said weakly.

"I don't have to prove anything. I'm Osiris. See-all, know-all god of truth, justice, and balloon artiste extraordinaire."

"Osiris…" Wilder repeated, looking wild-eyed.

"That's my name, don't wear it out," Osiris said flippantly. He turned, looking at Logan. "You two should get going. The investigation is over at the apartment. The cops have split. The two men this asshole sent in there after Seti will be blamed for your friend's death. Their death certificates will read 'natural causes.' Case closed. Consider it a fabulous parting gift for playing."

"Osiris, I don't know how to thank you," Logan said, smiling.

"Godiva chocolates. I'm partial to the creamy, truffle ones," Osiris grinned. "Seriously, don't thank me yet. I just put you back where you belong. But my brother is going to be seriously pissed off, and, as you know, he's inclined to hold a grudge." He turned to Wilder, who looked as though he was going to drop dead from a heart attack at any moment. "You know, I'm inclined to grant you your wish. A little payback for the headaches you've caused me." He waved his crook toward Wilder, who disappeared in a brilliant flash of golden light.

"What did you do to him?" Logan whispered, staring at the empty chair Wilder had so recently occupied.

"He wanted to be immortal. I granted him his wish."

"But…but he caused all of this!" Logan protested, shaking his head confusedly. "And you reward him by making him immortal? Do you know what kind of grief he's going to be free to cause now?"

"Nah. I made him immortal, sure…but I don't think he's going to cause anybody any more problems. Let's just say that when the museum finally returns Seti's sarcophagus to Egypt, it won't be empty," Osiris grinned mischievously. "Now, I've got to get going. Got an Underworld to run, you know. Have a nice life, you two. See you... eventually."

He winked out, leaving Logan and Seti alone in the office.

Groaning, Logan twisted his head from side to side, trying to work out the kinks in his neck. "I am going to seriously need a massage. I feel like I've been hit by a bus."

Seti smiled at him. "You will heal. You are strong, Logan. Stronger than I ever thought you would be. You stood against Setekh for me. I will never forget that. Although you should be thrashed for running away and leaving me behind when you came here after Wilder."

"Me? You fucking killed yourself to follow me!" Logan replied, giving Seti a slight push. "What were you thinking? Don't ever do that again, okay?"

"I would have walked through fire to get to you," Seti said earnestly. "But that is as it should be. You belong to me."

"That's something we need to work on," Logan said, folding his arms across his chest. The movement hurt too much and he let them fall back to his sides. "This whole ownership thing has got to go."

"You do not wish to be mine?" Seti asked. His smile crumpled into a heartbreaking hound dog expression that made something hot flare deep inside Logan's chest.

"I think that I want to be with you, Seti. Just not owned by you. There's a difference, you know?" Logan said, cupping Seti's cheek. "I'm not sure what I feel about you. Other than wanting to jump your bones as soon as the thought of moving doesn't make me cringe," he chuckled. "Maybe we can take it one step at a time, okay?"

"I cannot help feeling this way, Logan. When I look

at you I see a beauty in your eyes that I am lacking in myself. A gentleness. A sweetness. Your ka burns brighter than the sun, and I ache to bury myself in its warmth. It is why I claimed you as mine," Seti said softly. Seti's arms wrapped around Logan, pulling him in close.

As sore as he was, being held in Seti's arms felt good to Logan. Better than good. It felt right. He slid his arms around Seti's neck, reaching for a gentle kiss. "Let's go home, Seti. We'll stop at Jason's apartment first," he said, feeling the now familiar pang at the mention of Jason's name, "and then go over to my place. I think I need to sleep for a week."

Seti kissed him again, warm, lush lips pressing against his own. Seti's tongue swept over Logan's lips, tempting him to open. He did, and this time when the world spun away it was because Logan had lost himself in the taste of Seti, in the feel of those hands skimming soothingly over Logan's his back, in the hard muscles that pressed against him, and in the evidence of Seti's desire that ground into his hip.

"Not here, Seti," Logan whispered against Seti's lips. He leaned his forehead against Seti's, struggling for control. "I hate this office as much as I hate the man who owned it. I want to go home, to my own bed. It's not much, but it's big enough for two," he smiled.

"Then, we fly," Seti said, scooping Logan up into his arms. Logan protested, but secretly he admitted to himself that he sort of liked it when Seti went Tarzan on him. Made him feel wanted. Desired. Cared for. He wrapped his arms tightly around Seti's neck and squeezed his eyes shut.

As much as he trusted Seti, he didn't want to see what happened when Seti stepped out of the broken window on the 72nd floor of the Wilder Executive Tower and into thin air.

The wind bore them up, carrying them along cupped in its invisible palm, over the tops of the skyscrapers of Manhattan, affording them a spectacular view of the city. Or it would have, had Logan cracked his eyes open long enough to appreciate it.

Maybe someday he would, after he was more accustomed to riding the Seti Wind Express. For now, he was content to bury his face in Seti's neck and hold on for the ride.

They arrived at the apartment building in a much more sedentary fashion – through the back door. Seti had set them down in the alley behind the building. Taking a deep breath, Logan led Seti into the elevator for the long, creaking ride up to the fifth floor, and Jason's apartment.

What used to be Jason's apartment, Logan reminded himself, feeling a lump form in his throat again. Damn, going back in there is going to be hard.

Seti seemed to read Logan's thoughts, because he slipped his hand into Logan's, threading their fingers together reassuringly. Logan smiled up at him, grateful that he understood.

Chris and Leo were lost without their third wheel. They sat together on the coach, staring at the spot where Jason had died, their eyes red-rimmed. They looked almost surprised to see Logan and Seti when they walked in the door.

"Logan! Oh, thank God!" Chris cried, as they both jumped to their feet and threw themselves at Logan. "We thought you were dead, too!"

For the first time since Logan had known him, Leo was utterly silent. He pressed his face against Logan's neck, shaking and holding on for dear life.

"It's okay," Logan said, although at the moment it felt like anything but okay. "Everything will be all right. Look, you probably won't believe me, but I have it on excellent authority that Jason is happy. He's…well, he's a lot better off than any of us."

"Authority? Whose authority? He's dead, remember?" Chris snapped. Logan felt him tense, but just as quickly he slumped, as if someone had let the air out of him. "Oh, never mind. I'm sorry. I'm just…it's just so fucking hard, you know?"

"Yeah, I know, bud. I know," Logan said, although his heart ached anew.

Chris cleared his throat, backing away and swiping at his eyes with his sleeve. "What happened with Wilder? You did go to his office, right? Oh, my God, Logan… you're black and blue all over!" Chris cried, reaching for Logan's arm. He gingerly touched the red and blue bruises on Logan's forearm and throat that were starting to deepen into dark purple.

"Yeah, I did. I'm okay, though. It's a long story, and I'm really tired. Suffice it to say that Wilder won't be bothering us anymore," Logan said. He gave Leo another squeeze, before letting go and stepping back. His hand automatically searched behind him for Seti's. Finding it, he linked their fingers again.

It was odd how just the touch of Seti's hand calmed Logan. Reassured him. Logan wasn't sure what that meant, but he knew enough to know that he was going to find out.

"The police took the bodies…Jason's, too," Chris said. "I gave them the letter Perry had written you, Logan."

"Good. Then they know it was Wilder who caused all of this, although they're going to think Perry was crazy with all the talk about mummies and immortality. What about the arrangements for Jason? You know the…the funeral?" The word stuck in Logan's throat, coming out as a pained croak.

"Jason's parents are taking care of it. They said someone will call us to let us know," Chris said. He looked fragile, as if a tap on the shoulder would shatter him into a million pieces.

"Are you two going to be okay? We can stay awhile if you need us to..." Logan said, looking up at Seti and praying that he didn't argue. He didn't. He smiled at Logan and nodded, as if to say that he understood. He also hadn't made the slightest fuss when Chris and Leo had thrown themselves at Logan, kissing his cheeks and hugging him.

Damn. Maybe Logan didn't need to figure out what was going on between himself and Seti after all.

Maybe he already knew.

"Yeah," Leo finally spoke, looking down at his beat-up sneakers, as if not looking anyone in the eye would hide the fact that he'd been crying. "We're going to spend a couple of days at Wendy's. She called, made the offer. You know, figure out what we're going to do."

"Okay. We'll be at my place. I have my cell. Call me if you need anything, okay?" Logan said. "You two are welcome to stay there, too. Don't even hesitate, okay?" He turned to lead Seti out the door, but froze as his eyes fell on the spot nearby where Jason had fallen.

Fuck. This was hard. It didn't matter that Osiris had told him that Jason was happy and at peace. Logan knew without a doubt that every time he walked into that apartment – if Chris and Leo decided to keep it – he'd see Jason crumpled on the floor, his life ebbing out into a pool of crimson.

A strong arm draped over his shoulder, urging him out the door. He let himself be led outside, grateful again for Seti's strength.

CHAPTER TWENTY TWO

One year later...

"Oh! Oh, fuck yes!"

Seti had Logan bent over the kitchen table, plates and glasses half filled with juice rattling as he pounded himself into Logan's body. Again and again he thrust deeply, hitting what Logan called the "sweet spot" each and every time. Logan's husky voice swore a blue streak, his vocal encouragement nearly enough to send Seti over the edge.

Logan's body had never lost its appeal for Seti, even though they'd made love countless times over the last year. Not once in that time did Seti desire someone else. He doubted that he ever would. Every time with Logan was like the first time for him; he was continually finding new things about Logan, discovering new ways to please the man.

And luckily for Seti, Logan seemed to feel the same way. He was always ready for Seti, no matter what time of the day or night Seti decided to ravish him. This morning was a good example. The window in the kitchen had been cracked open, letting in a draft of chilly, fall air. They'd been in the middle of breakfast, enjoying the fluffy eggs and crisp bacon that Logan had made for them, along with large glasses of cold, fresh orange juice, when Seti had noticed that Logan's nipples had peaked in the cool air.

That was all it had taken. He'd reached out over the breakfast table, unable – and unwilling – to stop himself from touching Logan. His finger had circled Logan's nipple, rubbing and lightly tweaking the hardened bud. The next thing Seti knew, Logan's pajama bottoms had been pushed down around his ankles and Seti was buried up to the hilt inside of him.

Not that it was always Seti who initiated things. No, Logan did an equally fine job of that, and usually picked the most inconvenient times for it, too. He'd once dragged Seti behind a display of hubcaps in a dark corner of the automotive aisle at Wal-Mart, dropping to his knees and giving Seti a blowjob that was the stuff of legends.

Seti had gotten even with Logan the following week in the Anthropological Studies aisle at the New York City Public Library. Seti remembered Logan having to bite down on the spine of a copy of Darwin's On the Origin of Species to keep from screaming out loud when he'd come.

"Seti! Oh, God, Seti!"

"Not a god. Close, but not quite," Seti chuckled, angling himself and pushing in deep. Logan's hand was moving underneath his belly, the wet sounds of his hand on his cock sounding like the sweetest music Seti had ever heard. When he came, his entire body shuddered hard, contracting around Seti like a molten vise.

Seti threw his head back, howling his pleasure to the ceiling as he came, stars dancing in his peripheral vision. It was so good with Logan! No, it was better than good.

It was life, and Seti would never have enough of tasting it.

Breathing hard and still trembling from the strength of

his orgasm, Seti turned Logan around and drew the man in close, kissing Logan soundly. "You are my heart," he whispered. "Have I told you that yet?"

"Only about a million times. Not that I ever get tired of hearing it," Logan laughed. He laid his head on Seti's shoulder. "I love you, you know."

"I know," Seti said, feeling the lump form in his throat that always formed when Logan said those three powerful words to him. "But I never get tired of hearing it either."

He helped Logan clean up the mess they'd made, then helped him scrape the cold remnants of their breakfast plates into the trash.

For a five-thousand-year-old former Egyptian king, Seti thought he'd adapted well to twenty-first century living. He'd learned what a refrigerator, a stove, and a dishwasher were, and how to use them. Logan had taught him how to operate the dvd player (although he still couldn't set the clock on it – which Logan assured him was not at all unusual), the alarm clock, the toaster, and a myriad other mystical, magical household appliances.

He'd learned the monetary system, and how to read and write in English. Logan had taught him how to hail a cab, and how to figure out which bus and subway train would take him where he needed to go. Although he'd grown adept at using public transportation, Seti still used the Seti Wind Express, as Logan referred to his power over the elements, whenever he had the opportunity.

Hey, Seti thought, mentally shrugging his shoulders, you could only teach so many new tricks to an old dog.

The year had flown by swiftly. Logan had accepted Perry's old job as Curator of Relics, recently rechristened Antiquities and Curiosities at Logan's request. He was the youngest Curator in the Museum's history, and Seti was very proud of him.

Logan had published several papers over that time period, too, astounding theories – some quite controversial – about life in Ancient Egypt, and in particular, about a clan of nomads who called themselves the Children of Set. Try as they might, Logan's older colleagues couldn't discredit or dispute his findings.

Of course they couldn't. Logan had gotten his facts directly from the horse's mouth. His paper about the life and death of one King Seti had garnered him national prestige.

The first few weeks had been difficult for them. Logan had sunk into a black depression over Jason's death. They'd attended the funeral, which only seemed to drive home the point that his friend was not coming back.

It was then, sitting on the back steps of the funeral home as Logan had wept in his arms, that Seti had told Logan the full story of his Ashai. He had told Logan that he understood how it felt to lose someone you loved.

"You would have liked him, Logan. He was much like you – younger than I, smart. There wasn't an evil bone in his body," Seti had said, holding Logan tightly, stroking his hair. "I once thought that you were he returned to me. Now I know you are not him. You are unique."

"You loved him a lot, didn't you?"

"Yes. He was my heart. But I am a very lucky man, Logan. Geb has seen fit to give me another to replace the one I lost when Ashai died. He gave me you. You are also my heart. And you I will keep close to me all the rest of my days."

He'd kissed Logan then, his lips drying each of Logan's tears. Seti held Logan until he'd stopped trembling, rocking him back and forth.

Seti smiled to himself, remembering that at Jason's funeral there had been an enormous, beautiful bowl, carved with hieroglyphics and filled with blue and white Egyptian water lilies. The accompanying card had simply read, "O."

They'd both known who'd sent the flowers. Osiris.

Logan seemed to get a little better every day after that. It had been shortly after Jason's funeral that he'd first told Seti that he loved him.

Those three words never sounded sweeter than they had on Logan's lips.

"Hey," Logan said, snapping Seti's ass with the kitchen towel, "Penny for your thoughts."

"I was thinking of Osiris. And I worry that Setekh will seek revenge on us for shaming him as we did."

"We didn't shame him! He fucking shamed himself, Seti," Logan said, frowning. "He pulled every ounce of shit down on his own head."

"I know this. You know this. Osiris knows this. But somehow I doubt that Setekh knows this," Seti said, offering Logan a half smile. "It matters not. If he comes, we will face him together, you and I."

"Yeah," Logan said, reaching out for him. "You and I. I like the sound of that."

Seti smiled, enfolding Logan in his arms.

Outside the wind blew, kissing the window with frosty lips, as its master and his love raised the temperature inside.

Made in the USA